Karma

What comes around... Goes around...

The Anniversary Anthology

By

The Ladies of EyeCU Reading and Social Network

Ebony Evans

Sassy Satanya

B. Jackson

Rhena D. Holmes

M.L. Hawkes

Tam Telling Tales

Samaracheré

T. Denise

Kaylynn Hunt

For permission requests, contact the publisher at:
Skylar Publications LLC
Detroit, MI
 www.skylarpublications.com

Cover Design: Renee Wallace
Editor: T. Denise Black
ISBN: 979-8-9904480-3-2

First Edition
Printed in the United States of America

Introduction

Karma is more than a collection of stories—it's a celebration of sisterhood, storytelling, and the powerful journey of a book club that turned into a creative force.

Fifteen years ago, EyeCU Reading & Social Network began as a simple idea rooted in a love for books and meaningful conversation. Over time, it evolved into a dynamic, tight-knit community of readers who laughed, cried, and grew together—page by page. Now, in honor of our 15th anniversary, we proudly present our first anthology: *Karma*.

Each story in this collection explores the age-old concept of cause and effect—actions that demand answers, choices that ripple through time, and justice that arrives, sometimes quietly… sometimes with a vengeance. These tales of karmic retribution are as diverse as the women who wrote them yet bound by a shared passion for storytelling and truth.

For many of us, *Karma* marks our debut as published authors. It is a leap of faith born from encouragement, courage, and the unshakable support of our sisterhood. We hope these stories entertain, provoke, and resonate—and maybe even remind you that karma never forgets.

Welcome to our debut. Welcome to **Karma**.

~~ The Members of EyeCU Reading & Social Network

Forward

LOOK AT US NOW!

15 years strong. FIFTEEN! Rooted in our passion for Black literature, storytelling, honest reviews, and most importantly, in our love for one another. We didn't just build a book club.... We cultivated a sisterhood, a movement, and a community. We've cried together, laughed until we couldn't breathe, fell in love with fictional men (and wanted to fight a few), and turned pages into purpose.

EyeCU Reading blossomed into EyeCU Reading & Chatting, an online extension with 3.1K members and counting! Authors, readers, dreamers and doers. Freestyle Fridays became a whole thing. Tam Telling Tales? Iconic. We got a Freestyle Queen in the building, a professional editor, influencers, and yes.... WE ARE ALL PUBLISHED AUTHORS! What started with a shared love for books has become a shared legacy. This book, *Karma*, is a dream realized. But it's not just my dream. It's a 'we' thing. God did His part, and He surrounded me with you. My sisters, my circle, my hype crew, my safe space. Every author, every reader who's rocked with us on this journey… This moment belongs to you too.

Celebrating 15 years by hosting the EyeCU Reading Literary Experience powered by BRAE has been one of the most joyful and fulfilling experiences. And the cherry on top? Every member of EyeCU can now say they're published author. What book club you know doing THAT?! We are, and always have been, not your ordinary book club. And baybeee… If this is what the first 15 look like? I can't WAIT to see what's next.

With all my love,

Ebony

Visionary and President of EyeCU Reading & Social Network

Autograph Page

Karma

~

It's a fundamental principle of cause and effect, where actions (mental and physical) lead to consequences, which can be good or bad.

Table of Contents

Karma's A Bitch

By

Ebony Evans

You wanna know why Karma's a bitch?

Baby, sit tight, 'cause it started way before I ever took my first breath.

See, Karma ain't just some slick little payback fairy out here sprinkling bad luck like confetti. Nah. Karma was born from blood, built from bruises, and dressed in survival with a side of "try me if you want to."

I should know.

I am Karma.

And around here!

This ain't just my name ... It's my birthright.

Now, my mama, Destiny? She's the strongest woman I know, stitched together with spit, prayer, and pure uncut grit.

But her mama! Whew, chile! Hope McGraw? That name alone used to taste bitter on my tongue, like day-old Hennessy and regret. Hope was the type of bitter that could curdle cream just by breathing on it. Her name might've been "Hope" but don't let that fool you! She was about as uplifting as a cinder block to the chest and her spirit more dried-out than the wigs she kept lined up on the dresser.

She was named Hope because her own mama hoped she'd be a one-way ticket out the damn ghetto. Spoiler alert! She wasn't.

Instead of rising up, Grandma Hope marinated in her misery like a pot of greens left to simmer too long. Soggy, salty, and stinking up everything around her. Sure, she had looks. Mahogany skin, hips that could start fights, and a smile so sweet it could've led a preacher astray. But beauty ain't worth two dead flies when your soul's rotten.

Hope didn't just grow up hard... She grew up cold, raised by a woman meaner than a Detroit winter. And instead of melting that ice, she wore it like a fur coat—then wrapped my mama in it too.

You'd think a name like Destiny would carry hope, dreams, maybe a little light. Nah. Grandma Hope named her Destiny out of spite, swearing she was destined to not be shit. Imagine hating your own blood so bad you curse her every time you call her name. I heard the stories about how Grandma looked at my mama like she was something stuck to the bottom of her shoe. How my mama's soft curls, her light skin, her mismatched eyes... brown and hazel were daily reminders of everything Hope hated.

"You look just like your fuckin' father," she used to spit, like the words tasted like pennies and shit.

My mama caught more blows from words than most people ever did from fists. But instead of letting it break her, she made a vow... that if she ever had a daughter, she'd be everything her mama wasn't. And she damn sure kept that promise. She named me Karma. Because she said one day, I was gonna spin the block, right wrongs, and make the devil himself duck for cover. I ain't gonna hold you. I loved my name from day one. It made me feel chosen, like I was destiny's wildcard rocking Timbs, gold hoops, and a chip on my shoulder you could see from space. But let me tell you! A name like Karma doesn't come without a price. Mama poured every broken dream, every stolen hug, every unsaid "I'm proud of you" into me. She taught me the difference between being soft and being stupid. She taught me my worth before the world had a chance to cheapen it.

Hope?

She stayed gone.

No calls. No birthday cards. No fake-ass apologies.

And you know what?

We didn't miss shit.

Until that call came...

It was a Tuesday, and I was home after a long-ass shift at the clinic. Feet barking, wig slightly askew, ready to dive into some lemon pepper wings and catch up on *P-Valley*, when Mama's phone rang.

Her sister, Aunt Rhena.

I watched my mama's face tighten like a balloon right before it pops.

"They said she needs a kidney, Des. Can't find a match. I know you don't owe her nothing, but... I just thought I'd ask."

My mama didn't even blink, she just let out this long-ass sigh like she was exhaling twenty-something years of trauma.

"I'll think about it."

I was already shaking my head. "Mama, you don't owe her a damn thing. That woman's had a whole lifetime to fix her face and her ways. You did all this without her."

Mama didn't say nothing. She just stared out the window like she was watching ghosts dance on the sidewalk.

Next morning, she woke me up before the sun had even decided to clock in. She told me we were going to get tested.

"For what?" I mumbled, crust still in my eyes.

"For peace," she said. "Mine. Yours. Hers, maybe."

I didn't argue. Not 'cause I agreed, but because when Destiny makes up her mind, not even God himself can change it.

So, we went.

The tests came back three days later.

Mama wasn't a match. I was.

Let me pause right there. Because the irony? Delicious. I was the only person who could save the same woman who'd made my mama's life a living hell. The same woman who'd never even seen me. Never called. Never cared.

I wanted to say hell no on principle.

But something in me itched.

So, I threw on my scrubs, tied my curls into a slick bun, and marched into Hope Gaddis's hospital room like I was walking into a courtroom to give a verdict.

She didn't recognize me, of course. Too busy running that crusty mouth.

"These damn nurses get on my nerves," she mumbled, adjusting the pillow behind her like she was Queen Elizabeth. "And to think I wasted my good years raising a bitch-ass daughter. That bougie bitch think she better than everybody 'cause she got a husband and a big house. She ain't shit. Just like her daddy."

I froze.

Did this crusty old heffa just—?

She kept going.

"These young bitches work slow as hell. Look at this one—acting like she done seen a ghost. Just stupid. What the fuck are you staring at? Do what you gotta do and get the fuck outta my room."

I took a step closer. Let her get a good look at me.

"Hey, Grandma."

She squinted.

I smiled.

"It's me. Karma."

Karma's a Bitch

She stared at me like she was looking down the barrel of a loaded truth.

Her mouth twitched, but her pride wouldn't let her admit she was shook.

"You lyin'," she finally said.

I crossed my arms. "You wish."

She blinked slow. Studied my face. Her eyes went to my skin, then my hair, then my eyes…And that's when it hit her. My left eye, dark brown. My right? Hazel, just like her daughter's. The same mismatched pair she used to curse at when they stared back at her from a little girl's face.

"You Destiny's girl?" she asked, her voice catching.

"I'm the product of everything you tried to destroy," I said, cool as the other side of the pillow. "I'm the daughter of the woman you hated for being better than you. For surviving you."

Hope's mouth opened, but no words came out.

I leaned closer. "And guess what? I'm a match."

She sat up straighter now, like that meant something. Like life was handing her a second chance.

But I wasn't done. "Before you get your hopes up—let's get something straight. I came here outta curiosity, not compassion. I wanted to see the woman who made my mama cry herself to sleep. The woman who told her she should've been aborted. Who called her a mistake every damn chance she got."

Her jaw clenched. "You don't know what I been through."

"And you didn't care what she went through," I shot back. "You had a chance to break the curse, and instead, you passed it down like a family heirloom. Except we didn't want it."

She looked away. "I didn't ask for no visit. If you not here to help, then go."

I stepped back, folding my arms. "See, that's the thing. You don't ask for anything but still expect everything. Like the world owes you for the pain you handed out like party favors." She turned her head, but not before I saw the flash of something in her eyes. Regret? Maybe. Or gas. Hard to tell.

I walked toward the door.

"Wait," she said, voice dry. "So... you not gon' help me?"

I slowly turned. "You ever heard that saying... 'Karma always comes back around?"

She frowned.

"Well, congratulations. She finally did."

And I left.

***

Mama was waiting in the lobby. Her knee bouncing, eyes locked on the clock. She looked up when she saw me and stood. "How'd it go?"

I exhaled. "She's the same bitter broad she's always been. Still think she deserves a parade for surviving her own mess."

Mama nodded like she already knew. "You gon' do it?"

I tilted my head. "Would you want me to?"

"I want you to do what brings you peace," she said. "Because I already made mine." I smiled. That's what I love about her. She'd never ask me to carry a weight she put down years ago. But something about this didn't sit right…Something unfinished.

A week passed then two. I kept dreaming of hospital beds and broken women.

Finally, I made a decision. I showed back up at the hospital. This time, I was dressed in all black. Not for drama but for clarity.

I walked into her room. She looked worse. Shriveled. Quiet.

I pulled up a chair. "You got five minutes to listen. No interruptions."

She didn't argue.

I took a deep breath. "You had a shot at love, and you blew it. Twice. You hurt my mama so bad, she doesn't flinch anymore. That ain't strength…that's scar tissue. But you know what's worse? You could've fixed it. You could've picked up a phone, showed up, said sorry. But you didn't. And now, your time's up."

She stared at me like I was a ghost she wished would disappear.

I leaned in. "But here's the twist, Grandma. I did schedule the surgery."

Her eyes widened.

"Relax," I said. "You're not getting my kidney."

Confusion hit her face like a slap. "Then who?" I smirked. "Levi Holmes, the man you dragged through the mud. The one you said wasn't shit, would never be shit, and wasn't worth the air he breathed! The one you disrespected and swore wasn't worth a piss on fire!

Yeah, him.

My granddaddy.

He's your damn match.

And while you rotting in that bed, begging for another shot at life...

It's the man you hated most who's about to save it.

Not outta love.

Outta mercy.

And trust me, that's something you don't deserve. Let that marinate while you beg God for forgiveness."

She looked like she'd been punched in the gut. "He... what?"

Tears welled in her eyes. I stood. "That's real karma, baby. You ain't dying. Nah, that would've been too easy. You're gonna live every miserable day, knowing the same people you dragged through hell had to be the ones to drag your sorry ass back. Sit with that."

I headed to the door. Stopped. "You once told my mama she should've been swallowed. Maybe. But you? You should've choked." And I left. For good this time.

The surgery went fine. She lived. But that didn't mean she was forgiven.

Me and Mama? We thrived. Built generational peace. Turned pain into purpose.

People always say karma's a bitch like it's a bad thing. But sometimes, she's just a woman fed up, showing up, and shutting down generational curses like a boss. And if you ever wonder who she is...Check the mirror.

She might just be you.

THE END

Ebony Evans is the dynamic President of EyeCU Reading & Social Network, celebrated for her innovative ideas that help creatives shine. A devoted supporter of both emerging and established voices, Ebony is a pillar in the literary community and beyond.

In 2022, she made her author debut with the gripping novel *Dead to Me*, further cementing her place as a multifaceted force in the world of storytelling. A passionate reader, thoughtful reviewer, and self-proclaimed book nerd, Ebony infuses everything she does with enthusiasm and heart.

Outside of literature, Ebony is a devoted wife and mother who loves laughing, cooking, dancing, karaoke, and spending quality time with her close-knit circle of family and friends. Married since 2000 to her soulmate, Michael, the two share life with their spirited fur baby, Lacy, and their talented, high-energy daughter, Essence—whose vibrant personality and whirlwind of extracurriculars keep them busy and endlessly proud.

Life has taught Ebony the power of surrounding herself with like-minded, supportive people, and she brings that same compassion and encouragement to the spaces she creates. In all things, Ebony Evans remains a passionate advocate for community, creativity, and the transformative magic of books.

Karma, Unveiled

By

Sassy Satanya

Top of the day

"Thank you for waking me up, Lord! Millions didn't make it, but I was one of the ones who did!"

This is the grand rising gratefulness that Nicole woke up with every day. She would yell this out every single morning. No exceptions, no way, no day. She was raised to be grateful for all the good Lord provided to her. The only thing that could stop this praise is if Nicole actually were one of the millions that did not make it. After a restful night, she found her husband had already woken up and his side of the bed was chilled with a crispness that only the morning temps could leave on their satin sheets.

Nicole seemed to shake it off just like any other morning that Staten was not there when she woke up. This actually was nothing new. For someone who claims to adore her so much, Staten was always able to poke her with small daggers each and every day. I mean she did wake up at 3:12 every single morning. She had a regimen to meditate, exercise, shower and then start her day. You see, Nicole was on her own schedule full of discipline to complete her first series of many novels that she planned to write detailing a path of love, loss, and hope to regain it all back.

After the completion of all of Nicole's morning activities, she heard Staten calling her name while she was getting dressed.

"Nicole, my love, do you hear me?"

She finally decided to answer him.

"Yes, yes my love, I hear you!"

She was thinking, *how could I not.* However, she would never say that to him. She was a loving, respectful, and dutiful wife. At least that's how she wanted to appear. Her love for him had dissipated a long time ago. He just didn't know it, not yet anyway. She planned on letting him know soon though, very, very soon.

She was sure he wanted to know why breakfast was not prepared already.

Surprisingly, Staten stated that he brought breakfast home with him. A nice combination of avocado toast, fruit, and scrambled eggs.

Oh, she thought, *something different today.*

Eyes rolling so that he couldn't see.

"You're just getting in? I thought you were in the study doing some work or taking a meeting with one of your international clients."

As he kissed her on the forehead he said,

"No no no, I stayed at the office all night so as not to disturb you."

"How thoughtful." she said.

Cheating Motherfucker, she thought!

Once dressed and headed downstairs for breakfast she called her dearest and oldest friend, Chloe. She didn't answer. It just happens to be way too early for her to be up. Chloe didn't have as much discipline as Nicole. She was more of a free spirit. Chloe manipulated her schedule to accommodate her lifestyle which Nicole secretly admired. After all, it was 6:12am, why would Chloe be up this time of morning? The book release wasn't until 6 this evening so maybe she was ahead of the game already. After tonight, Nicole figured that she wouldn't have to worry about Staten's ass anyway so why should she bothered?!

Monique, Nicole's lead party planner, called to confirm the final details for the night. Every fine detail just had to be perfect. Not only was this night a lucrative business venture, it was also a new beginning for Nicole... in more ways than one. *It's good to have options even if you're not into all of them*, Nicole thought to herself.

Finishing up her call, she peeked in on her sleeping husband. She kissed him goodbye and left a sticky note on the nightstand.

See you tonight. Please don't be late. I have a surprise for you!

Nicole continued with final preparations for her super special day by getting her makeup done, some loose spirals in her hair and a quick polish change for her nails and toes. She went with a sexy French manicure for both. While at Prestigious Nails, her nail technician surveyed Nicole and made a strange observation.

"Hey, girl, you okay? You look a bit preoccupied, sad, worried or something. I can't put my finger on it, but something seems very different about you today."

"This is going to be one of the greatest nights of my life! I may just be a little nervous, but I am ecstatic! Make no mistake about it! I do, however, appreciate your concern. I will admit it would've been nice if I was hanging with my girl today, but I know how Chloe is... always dancing to the beat of her own drum," Nicole replied.

"Right. Right, your friend with the red Sisterlocks? I saw her last night leaving the club with some fine ass man. I bet she's still laying up with him if she is anything like me! Ha!! Like calling into work for the next day or two, okayyy! Only break I would have given ole' boy was to feed him so I could feed him again if you know what I mean. Keep that fine muthafucka on full 'cause babbbyyyy! I'm getting wet just thinking about his fine ass... Whew!"

Nicole shook her head in disgust listening to this raunchy bitch. She had no idea that this visit to Prestigious Nails would be her last visit to Prestigious Nails. Not only was this conversation unprofessional, it was also a damn lie. Nobody could tell Nicole that her bestie was a whore. Well, nobody used to be able to tell her that. But picking up some random man from a club that this raunchy talking nail technician would be at, Nicole didn't believe it. . She would like to think Chloe was better than that.

"I'm sure you are mistaken because Chloe wouldn't be picking up some random man at a club."

Nicole abruptly changed the subject, talking about her amazing night that was vastly approaching with the quickness. After promptly paying for and thanking the nail technician for her services, she sauntered out of Prestigious Nails headed to the suite she reserved to shower and dress for tonight's festivities. Nicole was thinking that she should have had a glam team on site. That way she could have avoided the type of awkward conversation she had just experienced. Nicole knew that day was coming very soon. After this book launch, she would be able to have a glam team whenever she wanted. For now, she'd focus on tonight. Tonight had its own important things to do like closing one door for the opening of another. After all, the book launch was actually a way of telling someone out loud that I know who you are!

The time was finally here. Nicole had been waiting for this night for months —many months.

She and her husband, Staten, were a match made in heaven. You know the type, every couple's favorite couple. Well, that was exactly how Nicole and Staten wanted to be seen. Each of them for very different reasons.

As all of the guests began to arrive, Nicole was gushing at how well the venue looked. Mocha this, mocha that, and the guests were to wear shades of cream, brown, and tan. Nicole hired the hottest up and coming party planners in town to collaborate on the launch of her new book...A tell all about her loving marriage. The who's who knew the prestigious couple in the most prominent communities and business circles that they ran in. Nicole and Staten were the talk of their town. Things could not have been more perfect. At least things seemed to be perfect to everyone else.

See, Nicole was tired of pretending. She wanted to live her life out loud. She didn't want to play Staten's game any longer. Only Nicole's editor, and her lead party planner, Monique knew the details of her book which would be exploding at this launch. Nicole had aspirations that surpassed being Staten's wife. It didn't matter how well he provided for them, the house they lived in, the expensive cars they drove, the luxurious places they vacationed or the lavish material things they'd accumulated; Nicole wanted true love.

Staten was the perfect husband until he was not. He was rich, well connected, came from a good family, and God fearing. Staten was basically a great catch. He could have chosen anyone, but Nicole was the apple of his eye. She was beautiful, a great homemaker, and the future mother of his children.

As Monique approached Nicole doing a shimmy, she asked, "Are you really ready to set it off today?"

"Absofuckinglutely!" Nicole responded.

"Okayyyy Girl! Let's do this shit!"

Once everything and everyone was in place, the newest published author of Sassy Publishing was introduced with a magical light show. The DJ played sensual songs— captivating the audience by creating a vibe like no other. Many onlookers were mesmerized by the beauty of the ambiance. Nicole was on a natural high feeling so exhilarated. It's as if the world was at a standstill. It's a moment in time she will remember for the rest of her life. A new beginning, a rebirth! Nicole's stories of love, loss, and healing were going to serve as purpose from her pain.

The venue was spectacular! Floral backdrops of fresh flowers with several displays that had yet to be unveiled. The idea was to build a bit of intrigue. Her guests would be anticipating what was behind the huge golden wrapped masterpieces. But those features had their time. They would be unveiled in sequential order from day one to current day.

Make no mistake about it, what is done in the dark will come to light this day. They will soon see... they will see what Nicole has known for days that turned into months. Everyone will see what, who, and why her life was making a dramatic change after tonight. They will have to see in full blown amazement just like her.

The creams, golds, tans, mochas, and shades of brown created a beautiful ambiance that was breathtaking to see. Nicole wore all gold from the top of her head adorned with a gold crown representing peace, clarity, and a deep understanding of her higher self. As she sashayed into the ballroom, everyone smiled and nodded with extreme admiration. She couldn't have been more pleased.

Once Nicole arrived at the podium, she directed the light show to slow down and then to stop completely. Her next direction was for the unveiling of the portraits showing small pieces at a time while she read excerpts from her book... bit by bit, slow and seductive, words of betrayal from her husband and best friend. Small details and quotes from their text and voice mail exchanges.

It was hard to hear the intimidate exchanges once the audience understood what was going on. The loud screams and gasps from friends and family showed just how much they despised the betrayal from Nicole's husband and best friend.

Chloe was devastated looking at the monumental portraits being unveiled while holding her new love's hand. Portraits taken of her & Staten in some very comprising positions. Taken in various places from hotel lobbies, coffee shops, five-star restaurants, and even at both of their homes. Nicole even displayed nude photographs that they thought were for their eyes only. Chloe never imagined being outed in such a public way.

It was Chloe all along, the woman with the red Sisterlocks leaving the club. The woman leaving with the "fine ass man" that the nail technician so eagerly described. Chloe never loved Staten after all. He was just a fantasy that she explored. Staten meant absolutely nothing to her. Nothing at all. Chloe had actually fallen deeply in love with that "fine ass man" but he now knows that Chloe ain't shit! Chloe watched him stare at those pictures of her and Staten in pure disgust before he walked out of the venue and her life and never looked back.

The one-man Chloe ever loved saw her naked in the arms of her best friend's husband. She stood there speechless for what seemed like an eternity because the man she loved did not utter a word on his way out.

Staten on the other hand, tried to explain himself.

"My Love, you got to be fucking kidding me?! I know this looks bad, very bad! My love for you has not changed, Nicole! I want you. I just want Chloe too! We can make this work."

Of course, Staten was shocked to all hell that Nicole knew his dirty little secret. He had been secretly courting Chloe for months. Initially, Staten made flirtatious advances towards Chloe that were never returned. He knew she was a bit on the wild side so whenever Nicole would have Chloe over for dinner or a casual movie or game night, Staten took advantage of the time they shared together. He actually cherished it. Maybe a bit too much because all he wanted was a chance to show both women that he was enough man for the both of them… at the same time.

After he convinced Chloe to meet him on one date, they then shared another. Soon after that, Staten had Chloe climbing the walls of the most exotic places they could find locally so as not to cause suspicion among his unsuspecting wife and her unsuspecting best friend. Unbeknownst to Staten and Chloe, Nicole knew about them after their first tryst because Nicole had him under surveillance. Call it women's intuition because a woman knows her man.

Without bothering to listen to his foolishness, Nicole sashayed out of the venue the same way she sashayed in, leaving the festivities in full force because this was news to the public and old news to her. Cameras flashing in Staten's face. Cameras flashing in Chloe's face.

Nicole had already mourned her marriage. Now it was Staten's turn. He could not have her. Maybe he could have Chloe but apparently not because here she is claiming to love the man she walked in with tonight. Staten had every intention of proposing a polygamous lifestyle for the three of them. He wanted to be married to both women.

His only devastation was losing them both.

It's funny how life can be.

"Why go through all of this to embarrass Staten and Chloe?" Monique asked.

"Karma's a Bitch!"

Before finally laying it down for the night, Nicole wrote one final thought in her journal...

Reward loyalty with loyalty

And

Reward disrespect with distance

Sassy Satanya is the newest member of the EyeCU Reading & Social Network—having joined just 14 short years ago! A proud mother of two, she lives in the suburbs of Detroit and has worked in quality control in the auto industry for nearly three decades. *Karma* marks her first foray into publishing, with many more writing projects on the horizon. She credits her book club sisters for inspiring her creativity and encouraging her to step far beyond her comfort zone.

A Debt Called Karma

By

B. Jackson

Prologue

Dr. Tron Ford

THEY SAY KARMA IS A BITCH AND I GUESS
THEY WERE RIGHT!!□

Waking up in a box in downtown Detroit is surely not how I imagined my life, but here I am. How did I fumble my life and my wife? Who would have thought going from a huge house, beautiful, educated wife, wonderful kids and a medical practice as a fertility doctor that was envied across the state, that this could be my new reality. Like they say, never take anything for granted. Most importantly, don't take your wife and the life you've built together for granted.

Well, I guess you're wondering how I got here. The words that come to mind are selfishness, narcissistic, and downright disloyal landed me in this damn box. Ten years had slipped by since I first opened the doors to my practice in Beverly Hills as one of the most sought out fertility doctors in Michigan. People traveled near and far just to be the patient of the famous Dr. Ford. I had helped many couples start a family. Many of whom had tried just about everything to conceive and although my services were far from what I would call affordable, I still never had an empty appointment slot. To top it off, the wait list was full of waiting families whose fate I held in my hands. My schedule consisted of late nights and early morning and even when I was done with work, somehow there was always some reason not to go home.

Looking back, I realize I should have been a better husband, father, person and doctor. I was close to celebrating my 20-year wedding anniversary, and yet my focus was so far from my home life. Even if I tried, I could not blame that on just my practice. I was a complicated man and the life I chose was so complicated that I could barely keep all my wrong doings straight.

Chapter 1

The Beginning

Tron Ford

My wife Londyn and I met in Grad school at Wayne State University. We both set goals to have a career in the medical field. It had been a long day of class in one of our many lecture halls we shared. I never really noticed how beautiful she was. I always seemed to have my eye on someone else, but that's a story for a different time. This particular evening, I was emotional and physically exhausted. The day had taken its toll on my mood, going home without finding some relief did not seem like a viable option. I attempted to look around for my friend. I was hoping I could persuade them to have a hang out session, but the room was empty and just myself, Londyn, and Professor Gillian were left in the lecture hall.

That's when it hit me, this girl was beautiful and had already proven to be smart as hell. Standing at 5 ft 7 inches, dark skin tone, and ass and titties that could make a grown man cry. My options for the night had just looked up. Looking at her lips and then her sexy brown eyes, I made my first attempt at small talk.

"Hi, I'm Tron. It seems we were left behind tonight."

"I guess everyone else got out of this room as quick as possible."

"Yes, it seems that way. Today was a long day for me so mentally, I needed to pace myself".

"I can relate. It took me some time to get my bearing and prepare to leave as well."

"I noticed you did not give me your name. Was that as intentional as it feels. I think my feelings may be hurt."

"Stop it. Tron there is no need to be dramatic. Where is your friend tonight? I figured you all would be headed out to the nearest bar. I am quiet, but I do pay attention."

"Well, it seems it's just us."

"I tend to stay to myself. It always seems to keep my life simple and my studies my focus."

"Well, you have a great night."

"You as well, Mr. Tron."

"Soon to be Dr. Tron Ford."

"If it's okay with you I'll wait until it's official."

"Again, enjoy your night."

If I didn't know any better, I would say she knows something about me that I don't. The way

Londyn brushed me off hurt my pride a little. She even called me dramatic. Although I could be at times, there is no way she could know that. I can't help but wonder why she gave me the cold shoulder. Maybe she truly just wants to concentrate on her studies, but look at me, standing at 6 feet 5in, dark chocolate skin, big feet, and trust I could hang a pair of jeans, even If I had to say so myself, I was a catch. I was not used to rejection and I was not ready to get used to it. I thought to myself, we will meet again. I would make sure of it.

Suddenly, I flashed back to a peer calling her rich girl. Was that the reason she blew me off? Is it obvious I'm not well off and neither is my family? I guess it's time to move on. These thoughts are for another day. Tonight however, I needed a stress reliever, and I needed it fast.

Chapter 2

Londyn Price

As I headed to my car in a rush to get home, I had to laugh at my run in with Tron. He exuded cockiness and boy was he fine. I had no interest in being caught up in his web. He was either leaving with his boy from our class or smiling in the face of some woman. Either way, I was focused on completing my master's program so I could move toward the next steps to becoming Dr. Londyn Price. Although I was financially secure, I wanted to show my parents that I could earn a good living on my own. However, for now, I have a beautiful River Front Condo, a Mercedes G Wagon, all my expenses and college paid for by Mr. & Mrs. Price of Price Consulting Firm.

Price Consulting is a Tech Firm that specializes in creating software for most mobile phone carriers. It has become quite lucrative over the years. My parents started the firm back when we were just a figment of their imaginations. Myself and my brother Lennox, did not wish to walk in their shoes, because we both had our goals and careers focused on working in the field of medicine.

My brother was a bit of a hot head, impatient, and indecisive. He, at first, had his goals set on becoming a doctor as well, but he was always very abrupt in his decision making and quickly gave up those goals to pursue his BSN. In his own words, "I need to make money now and find my happily ever after. I don't want to attend five more years of school." I thought he had just given up, but I have learned throughout the years to just let Lennox do Lennox. He never appreciated my advice, so I stopped trying to influence his choices.

Most people would find it hard to believe we are identical twins, yes identical. I often question it myself. My parents love to confirm it for me. They reported they had been attempting to have children for many years without success and decided to consult a fertility doctor. The doctor helped them conceive and have a healthy pregnancy after a long wait. From that pregnancy, Lennox and I were born. He now has a pretty successful career as a nurse, but according to him he still needs to land a lucrative position at a private practice that can really benefit him and allow him to flourish as a nurse.

For as long as I can remember, my brother has always been competitive and waiting for his big come up. I often worried about his never seeming satisfied in his career. Though we were close, his competitiveness sometimes caused conflicts. It was nothing a little distance couldn't solve. Distance makes the heart grow fonder; I hope. Either a break from home was needed sometimes or just a break from Lennox. His leaving college early and going the BSN route gave us the space I felt we needed. Absence truly did make my heart grow fonder for my little brother. I was 59 seconds older and made sure he knew it. All in all, I was very proud of him. He had accomplished his most immediate goals and was making well over six figures as a nurse.

Well, I went walking to my car with thoughts of my brother. We had really become even closer during my last years of my medical program. We talked daily and sometimes multiple times a day.

As I was daydreaming and rushing to my car to get out of the school parking lot, I was in complete shock when I realized my window on my truck was down. Panic hit me as I imagined how I could have made this mistake when rushing into class. That's when I noticed the glass on the ground. My window wasn't down; it had been broken. An immediate fear rushed me as I remembered my handgun was left in my car safe. I prayed it was still there. As I got in the vehicle and searched under my seat for my safe, I realized the thieves must have had a time trying to detach the safe. There were scratches and dents where they surely tried. As I lifted my head back up. I was startled by the man standing at my door. A scream left me before I could process the face of Tron as the shadow in the dark.

Tron immediately panicked and apologized for scaring me. He explained, he thought I needed help once he saw my rear tire was deflated. First, I thought he was mistaken. I surely had not noticed. I got out and then the second shock hit me. Not only had my car been broken into, but the thieves had also flattened a tire as well. They must have been pissed they could not get that safe out of the truck. This night is becoming more exhausting as each minute passes. I am so over it.

Calling Triple A was pretty much a lost cause, because the 3-hour wait was time and patience I did not have. Tron was still waiting patiently to ensure I made it home safe. He was laying it on thick. I assumed his ultimate goal was to gain my attention. He surely did not like my dismissal of him earlier before we left class. Here he comes up to my truck again.

"Hey, what did Triple A say?"

"Well, it looks like it's going to be at least 3hours before they can come to help me."

"I will sit here and wait with you, but I think I should know the name of the person I'm dedicating my time to."

"Maybe we should start over."

"That sounds great," Tron spoke with no hesitation.

Chapter 3

Tron Ford

I think I finally got Londyn's attention. Well at the very least, she was no longer blowing me off and she even seemed to be enjoying my company. I had suggested we sit in her back seat while we waited for help to arrive. This way if she needed to nap, she would be more comfortable. I think the real intention was to not be separated by the center console in her truck and really be able to get cozy. Before I realized it, one hour had passed and we had been talking the entire time. I had disclosed that my dad was also a doctor when I was growing up, but due to a malpractice lawsuit, we had pretty much lost everything. As if that was not enough, I had lost my mom to cancer a few years later. I really think the stress of my dad's legal trouble played a huge roll in her transitioning so quickly. A part of me always wanted to blame him, but he was the only parent I had left, and I needed and wanted him to remain a part of my life. I learned to forgive him and together we built a good bond over the years.

I asked Londyn what she planned to specialize in as a physician, and she explained her goal was to be a plastic surgeon. Londyn said she always dreamed of helping people become the very best they could be and that is how she planned to do it. I was asked the same question, and I explained my goal was to be one of the most sought-out fertility doctors in this country. I planned to work my butt off to achieve this goal. For a slight moment, I think I saw Londyn smile. Londyn for once seemed to be impressed by something I shared. I don't know how she was feeling after an hour, but I could not think of a better way to spend my Friday night. We continued to chat, and Londyn was getting sleepy as the minutes passed. I could tell exhaustion had taken over her body. She became less engaged and was barely talking. She leaned back into her seat as we continued to share and before either of us knew it, she had fallen asleep. But I made sure she landed comfortably in my arms. It felt great to be holding her. Especially since earlier, she didn't even want to share her name. I began to relax in the moment and soon we both passed out, me holding her and her lying in my arms.

I was so pissed when I heard the knock on Londyn's car window. I knew it had to be Triple A or trouble. I didn't feel prepared for either.

"Hello, I am Kobe from Triple A, I'm sorry to startle you. I am just here to help," he spoke.

Londyn explained the issue to her truck and the driver suggested it be dropped off at the Mercedes dealership since it was missing a window and all. He asked Londyn if she had a way to get home. I spoke up and told Londyn I could drop her off if she did not mind me knowing where she lived. She did not see any issue with my taking her home. As a matter of fact, she explained a cup of coffee might do me some good before I decided to take the long drive back to my side of town. We had talked about where I lived as we chatted. She was not far from Wayne State University being in a condo in Downtown Detroit right near the Riverwalk.

Chapter 4

Londyn Price

My mind wandered the entire time we drove toward my condo. Waking up in his arms was surprisingly pleasant. Where did he come from? I had to ask myself, because I knew I was not prepared, nor could I afford to have any distractions. I'm inviting him for coffee before he drives home. We were both exhausted from the day's events. We were finally arriving at my condo. I told Tron to pull in my driveway, and he obliged. I gathered my books and things from his car.

"How will you get around tomorrow with no car?" he asked.

I explained I would be renting a car first thing in the morning. I asked Tron if he was still interested in coming in for coffee and of course he said yes. There was no way I was getting rid of him that easy. We made our way to the front door, and I entered the code to let us in. From the time we walked in, he was in awe of my beautiful space. I decided to take him on a tour. Once he saw my place, I told him to have a seat, and I proceeded to the kitchen to make some coffee.

Looking at the clock, I noticed it was already after eleven o'clock. We had been out of class for hours already. He had truly been a good sport. He made the decision to be present during my time of need, for which

I am grateful. We both hurried through a cup of coffee and the conversation picked up where we left off before I fell asleep. I mean, this man really was a whole vibe, but could he be trusted? I still had my doubts. Somehow, we went from coffee to wine and the vibes were still going strong.

I had the brilliant idea to play a game of truth or dare once the wine had me feeling risky. We flipped a coin to determine who would ask the first question and just like that, things went left. The coin flipped in his favor and then the night heated up. He wasted no time asking the first question. I chose a dare of course, again the wine.

Tron said, "I dare you to kiss me."

Just like that, we were kissing right in my family room, and it was the most amazing kiss I'd ever had. It had me warm in all the right places. Once it was my turn to challenge him, he chose a dare as well. At this point I was feeling challenged by him and I just love a good challenge. It felt like minutes had passed since I had spoken his dare, but it was mere seconds before Tron was up my skirt pulling down my panties and meeting my clit with his tongue. Yes, I was bold enough to dare him to go down on me. OMG! I had no idea how much pleasure he could offer; I was not disappointed. There was no looking back at this point.

Before I knew it, we were in a full fledge oral sex session. I was enjoying every minute of it. This man was amazing, and I could not get enough of him. I quickly went from being the snack to snacking on him and I'd never had anything that tasted this good. The real test would be what kind of lover he would be. Before I could finish the thought in my head, he was entering me. I knew I should stop him to ask about protection, but I was too into the moment to pause. We were not only engaging in sex, but it was unprotected sex.

I am positive I knew better than this behavior. The sex session went on for at least an hour and each time he entered me it felt like something brand new and amazing. He knew all the right spots and he left no stone unturned. This man was rocking my world, and I was loving it. I had already cum twice and was still waiting on him to explode. Let's just say he took his time. When the time came for him to finally cum, he pulled out just in time to explode on my chest. It was warm and mesmerizing.

The next morning was all a blur. Waking up to Tron was shocking yet felt comfortable. We both woke up at about the same time.

"Good morning, Londyn, I hope I did not invade your space for too long."

I answered him explaining his company has been a pleasure and my space did not feel invaded at all. I followed that up saying I think we should talk. Tron was saying the words as well at the very same moment. I offered to have the conversation over breakfast and asked if he could drop me off at the rental car company once we left breakfast. He of course agreed. We had a great breakfast and tried to discuss what happened last night and what it meant for us today. We agreed to just take things one day at a time and that's what we did.

Tron took me to get a rental car and had to follow me back home as he had forgotten his cell phone at my house. Before we knew it, we were again in a full fledge sex session. This time there were no doubts in my mind that I wanted all he had to offer.

Chapter 5

Tron

My life had been a whirlwind lately. Months had passed since I first met Londyn Price, and during most of that time, I stayed at her home. I'd practically moved in and only went back to my house I shared with my dad to grab some of my things. Things were great. I wouldn't say I was dating her exclusively, but we surely had something special. I knew I needed to cut ties to a couple of loose ends and soon I surely would. There are some things about me Londyn will never know and other things she thinks she knows. It goes back to why she wouldn't give me her name during our first encounter. Anyway, things were moving in a great direction and we both had finished school and started our residencies at local hospitals in the Detroit area. I never quite understood why Londyn worked so hard. I mean she is already rich and does not need to make a living, but she insisted on not living off her parents but completely building a life on her own with the money she earned. Me on the other hand, I had nothing since my dad's malpractice lawsuit had wiped his bank account out. Between the legal fees and the settlement he had to pay, it was like his being a doctor was of no benefit.

2 Years Later...

I had been happily married to Londyn for a year. I was due to start my own medical practice any day now. I had received a lot of help from my dad's connections that had almost made the process seamless. Of course, I had to ask Londyn for some financial help, which she agreed to without any push back. I could not be more excited. This should have been a time when we were both starting our own practice. Things had changed for us drastically and one of our dreams would need to be put on hold. We both agreed those dreams would be Londyn's. At seven months pregnant, she did not seem to mind. One of us would need to be at home with the newborn baby and realistically we couldn't realistically both be out of the house all day and night to get a new medical practice off the ground. She had fallen on the sword. So, I allowed myself to chase my dreams. It felt selfish, but I had always been a little me, my, I anyway.

Two months later we had a baby boy and almost one year after that we welcomed a daughter who was the spitting image of Londyn. Life was moving fast, and my practice was doing better than I had ever expected. I had learned so much from my dad about running a practice and it had given me a leg up to succeed. Londyn's practice was still on hold, but she never really seemed to complain. She was genuinely happy my practice was going so well. I wasn't sure I deserved her, but I was happy to have her. Since we had been married, I had been on the straight and narrow. Temptations and old sex interest had been left behind. I was a good husband and planned to stay that way. My father was enjoying having input into my practice and at times I allowed him to assist so he could still experience the life he had lost. I did tell him all dealings with my practice had to be above board. No funny business would be allowed. He was not actually innocent in his legal issues. He was not allowed to treat patients, but nothing said he couldn't work in a doctor's office.

I'll never forget the shock we had while introducing our parents.

"Dr. Ford is that you?" It was Londyn's dad who said it first.

My dad immediately answered, "Yes." Londyn's parents were very emotional, and I was unsure why. Londyn's dad began to explain my dad was their fertility doctor that helped them have their two beautiful kids Londyn and Lennox. I was in a state of shock. Londyn was even more shocked. What are the chances that the world could be this small? My mind immediately wandered off with questions, and I knew I needed to have a conversation with my dad as soon as time permitted. This could've been either a bad ending or a beautiful coincidence.

My dad had been charged with fathering children of his patients to ensure he never failed at delivering the couples the kids they were indeed trying to have. To say he took his job too seriously would be an understatement. According to my dad, he had not engaged in indiscretions with The Price family and his methods as their fertility doctor were successful and they eventually became pregnant. Something in his sad eyes made me want to question him more, but I trusted my dad even when others did not.

Chapter 6

Lennox Price BSN

I am still in shock. I can't believe after all this hard work I put into becoming a great nurse, I had now lost my job. I was employed at this clinic for eight years working under Dr. Simp. I worked so hard at everything I did. I knew I was a great nurse. I was dating another male nurse that also worked at the clinic and life was good. One day Dr. Simp asked me to increase the cost of a procedure, which would inflate the price the procedure should cost. After many questions, I decided to obey his orders. I really gave it a lot of thought, but I figured he knew what he was allowed to charge. As time passed, I was inflating numbers more and more and charging insurance companies more than what they should be paying us.

I didn't complain anymore because the kickback I was receiving from Dr. Simp was keeping my bank account larger than my normal pay even came close to. One day my boyfriend overheard what me and Dr. Simp were up to, and he immediately questioned our integrity and told me he never wanted to see me again. I was left broken hearted, but the status of my bank account allowed me to think everything was okay. My ex eventually quit the clinic. He refused to be guilty by association, and I was too dumb to follow suit or to care.

I was making more of my own money than Mrs. Londyn and that was always a goal of mine. My sister was still playing the dutiful housewife. I never thought I would see her like this. She seemed happy and I hoped her happiness was not an act.

Today I needed my sister, but how was I going to explain all of this to her? The clinic I worked at was being investigated and all the staff had been let go. Dr. Simp was not allowed to practice until the investigation into his books were completed. I knew he would never practice again, but that reality had not sunk in for him. I just prayed that in some way, I would be able to just walk away, even after the investigation was concluded. I would not even take calls from Dr. Simp. The police or whomever would have to show up at my house before I spoke again on Dr. Simp or any of his patients.

It was six pm, and instead of heading home, I decided to make my way to my sister's house. Londyn could tell immediately I was upset. She told me to let her put the kids down and then we could chat. While I waited for her return, Tron came in the door. We kicked it for a bit while I waited for Londyn's return. He was always super friendly whenever I saw him. Today was no different. He decided to share how great things were going for him. This was also the norm, but I didn't mind. He explained his fertility clinic was doing great and he had customers coming from out of state just to see Dr.

Tron Ford. He was ecstatic to walk in his dad's footsteps, and I felt his excitement.

Londyn soon appeared again, and she asked if we needed to talk in private. I explained Tron being there was okay. I proceeded to tell her how I lost my job. I explained that Dr. Simp was being investigated for insurance fraud, and they had to close the clinic. I failed to admit I was also helping Dr. Simp commit insurance fraud. I didn't think giving her that information would be helpful to me, so I omitted it from my explanation of why I'm here. It sounded much better for me to be the victim. I mean I was kind of a victim, right? The transgressions were not of my doing; I was just following orders. Knowingly knowing they were wrong, but still just obeying the doctor. Before Londyn was able to form a response, Tron's interest was piqued.

He immediately asked me, "Are you looking for a new job right away, I may have something for you."

Londyn sighed, but she didn't say anything.

"Are you serious, are you offering me a job?" I asked Tron.

"Yes, the office has picked up and I could use an additional nurse."

"I will take it," I quickly replied.

Just like that I was now a nurse at the fertility clinic of Dr. Tron Ford. I am sure that meant seeing a lot more of my sister. After Tron headed upstairs for a shower, my sister made it a point to say, "Next time we should talk in private."

I didn't really know why, but she did not seem happy I would be working at the clinic with Tron. I paid her no mind and was in celebration mode. Londyn did agree to have a shot with me to celebrate. Maybe I was reading her lack of happiness wrong. After all she celebrated with me.

Chapter 7

Dr. Londyn Price

For some reason my day now felt off. I loved my brother, but him working for my husband just didn't seem like the best idea. I know it may not make sense, but they just didn't seem like a connection that anything good could come from. My brother could be a lot, and my husband was so full of himself, he forgot what it meant to be humble. I mean I love Tron, but I do see a difference in his behavior sense he has become so successful. I know I sacrificed my career, so maybe that gives me some doubts as well. I don't know, they just aren't a match made in heaven in my eyes.

A few years have passed since Lennox has been working with Tron. They both seemed super happy with the arrangement. They surely had erased any doubt I had about them working together. There days working have gotten longer. Tron leaves for work around 8 am and very seldom gets home before 8 pm. Some nights he even goes out opposed to coming home to his wife and kids. It sometimes feels like I'm a single parent. Financially we couldn't be better, but I was feeling a little emotionally abandoned by Tron. I can even add sex starved to that equation. We went from not being able to take our hands off each other to barely taking time out for sex.

I feel Like I was missing out on a huge part of his life, but most importantly, I was missing out on a huge part of mine. Goals had been postponed, and I moved right into the dutiful supportive wife. I expected to be back to work by now for sure. Even if starting a practice was too much right now with two small children; I surely did not go to medical school to sit at home. This is exactly why I wanted to stay focused and not start a relationship when Tron suddenly fell into my lap. Well, there is no need to cry over spilled milk, but I swear I truly need some adult outlets.

I think it's time my parents had some overnight guests for the weekend. I can call my girl Khloe and we can go out. She is free of kids and a man. She is always ready for a good time. That's exactly what I needed. As soon as I picked up the phone to call my parents to ask if the kids could stay the weekend, my phone rang.

"Hey Tron."

"Hey Honey, I was calling to let you know me and Lennox were going to go out for some drinks after work."

"Do you ever stop to think that I may have plans Tron?"

Of course, his response was one of disregard and carelessness as he stated, "Since when do you have plans?"

"Me and your brother need a pick me up after the patients we had to deal with today," he continued.

All I could muster up was, "Whatever Tron. You enjoy your night out as always, by the way, the kids are fine!"

I called my parents, and an hour later I was kid free and ready to have a night out. I didn't waste time checking in with Tron or even updating him on the kids. I am sure it would not be high on his priority list to care. Dr. Tron Ford has proven to be very ME, My, I lately. Even hearing from Lennox was a thing of the past. I guess he forgot I was his sister and Tron was my husband. It was like their relationship had truly erased my existence. I thought about mentioning it to my parents and thought better of it. They would be talking for the next 10 minutes about how that brother of mine needs to settle down again with a nice man. Oh well, enough about them for the night. I knew there was no chance the two of them were sitting up in a bar thinking about me, so why am I thinking about them?

Chapter 8

Dr. Tron Ford

We were wrapping out the last patient and both me and Lennox were fit to be tied. I knew he would enjoy a night out as much as I would. I truly enjoyed his company. I don't know if it was him or the fact he reminded me so much of Zion, an old friend of mine from college. I missed him, but he cut all ties with me once I started dating Londyn.

He stopped even acknowledging me while we were in class. We went from hanging every other night to not at all. I must say I miss his body and the things he used to do to my body. Lennox reminds me so much of him. His build and personality are almost identical to Zion. I've often thought about looking him up but thought better of it. After all, I am a married man with a family. Lennox walked back in after walking out the last patient and I could see the exhaustion of the day weighing him down. I watched him closely while wrapping up my thoughts about Zion. I tried to laugh off my thoughts with small talk.

"Bro are you really that tired? Maybe you shouldn't have been hanging out last night with your friend and you would be well rested."

Lennox sat down in the chair in my office as he laughed and playfully said, "If I didn't know any better, I would say you sound jealous."

I wasn't sure how to reply. I wanted to play it safe. I simply said, "What if I was?" Lennox looked shocked and delighted at the same time. I felt nervous once I completed the sentence. I think I may have gone too far to turn back now. Lennox came closer to where I stood and asked, "Now what reason would a happily married man have to concern himself with what I am doing outside of work?"

He sat down in my office chair while waiting for my reply.

"Well, I guess it could have been time you spent with me."

"I don't think you are interested in taking my stress away like he does after work," Lennox quickly said.

"Maybe not, but I sure could release some stress after work too. My family is usually sleep when I get home."

Lennox didn't reply to me this time. He just stared at me with a devious smirk on his face. I was scared to speak again. I sat pondering how to remove the awkward silence. The silence seemed to be the loudest noise I'd ever heard, and it was making me second guess the last few minutes. Had I upset Lennox? Would he tell Londyn about this conversation? Lord, what is he thinking right now?

Is this what drowning felt like? As weird as this night was getting, I finally noticed my dick had become rock hard in his silence. Was this the reason he was no longer talking? I moved around in my chair to attempt to reposition myself, but the hardness was too stiff to adjust. I tried to think about something other than Zion and Lennox and that proved to be impossible as well. I had to sit there in the moment we had created and live with the words I had spoken.

Chapter 9

Lennox Price BSN

I was asking myself in my head, is this really happening? Is my brother-in-law flirting with me? Was I flirting with him? Watching him look so uncomfortable was hard. I wanted to let him off the hook but taking advantage of this moment sounded a lot more fun.

Abruptly I asked, "Is your dick hard, Tron? Let me see it."

If he could turn red, he would be right now. I half expected him to excuse himself from my presence, but instead he stood up and dropped his pants and briefs and sat back down in his chair. My mouth fell wide open at the beautiful piece I saw. I mumbled to myself, "This is why my sister is happy being a housewife."

I walked over to Dr. Ford, wondering if he would take cover and he did not. My brother-in-law was standing at attention and I needed to taste him. I did just that. One thing led to another and by the time we left the office we had both relieved some stress. It was some of the most amazing sex I ever had.

It felt like an immediate connection. One that didn't feel familiar to me at all. I wasn't one to be attached to a man. I usually just used them for moments of passion but nothing too serious. Now my sister's husband had the nerve to be the exception. I wanted his dick again already and we had only been done giving ourselves to each other just moments ago. The love making was magical. I had so many questions for Dr. Ford. I need to know why me. I asked him just that.

He simply said, "Why not, you?"

I didn't say it, but I surely thought, because I'm your brother-in-law. I refused to say anything that could possibly make him have regrets. I kissed him instead. I explained how wonderful our love making was and we prepared to leave like always and head to a local bar. The big difference today was, we were hand in hand walking out the door.

This night had surely been a strange turn of events, and I was smiling from ear to ear. It's not that I don't love my sister because I do, but I don't think I introduced anything new to her husband. There is no way he took me in all his holes and took me in all mine without any experience with a man. There is just no way! It doesn't make my actions right, but no one can say I introduced being with a man to Dr. Tron Ford. Being with a man was very familiar for him. Either way, this night has surely started off amazing.

We made it to the bar and Tron insisted that we get the VIP section in case we wanted to talk. All I wanted to do at that moment was dance. Instead, I followed Tron's lead and to the VIP section we went.

Once we were settled, Tron decided we should talk. I agreed.

"This can't happen again. I love your sister," was what he led with.

I could not help but think, *you sure have a funny way of showing it.* Those words were only in my thoughts. I had no desire to make him feel bad. I was sure he already did. Instead of responding to his statement, I asked, "Is this your first time being with a man?"

"No." Tron responded quickly.

He explained he briefly dated a man while in medical school.

"Are you gay?"

"I didn't think so, but I loved being with you so maybe I am."

"Do you really believe that was it for us?" I questioned.

And before he could even answer I explained.

"Life is meant to be lived one day at a time and today was our day one. Whatever happens moving forward, happens."

I quickly tried to lighten the mood as Kendrick Lamar's "They Not Like Us" boomed through the speakers. First, I did a light crip walk, and then I grabbed Tron's hand and dragged him to the dance floor. We vibed out the rest of the song.

Chapter 10

Dr. Londyn Price

I got to Khloe's house to pick her up at about 11:00. I had already been on the other side of town to drop off my kids. I refused to stay in and relax. I needed a grown-up night, and I was going to get one. We made it to the club and thankfully, the valet was still open. I hated to walk a long distance in heels, so this worked out great. I was sure Khloe appreciated the valet once I saw the high heels she was sporting. We looked great even if I had to be the judge and jury. We walked in and the party was already lit. The DJ was playing Kendrick Lamar's "They Not Like Us" and we walked in and found an open table and sat down before someone tried to claim it. We immediately ordered a round of drinks. A Lemon Drop for myself and a Dirty Martini for Khloe. That was truly her signature drink. We waited for our drinks while we watched the dance floor.

I quickly noticed two fine brothers dancing and vibing to the music having a great time. They seemed so delighted it made me laugh. As I continued to watch them, I realized it was Tron and Lennox. For some reason, I immediately felt strange. Not that two men couldn't vibe out together, but for some reason I felt an instant cloud come over me. I smiled as I headed to the dance floor. The song was quickly coming to an end. I decided to head back to my seat at that moment.

I watched as Lennox and Tron headed back upstairs. They were in the VIP area living it up. After our drinks came, I decided to walk upstairs to the VIP area to greet my brother and my husband. To say they were shocked to see me was an understatement. They damn near jumped out of their seats. I couldn't tell if they were shocked I was in a bar or if there was something else. No one rushed over to give me a hug. They stared at me awkwardly for some time.

Tron finally said "baby, what are you doing out?"

I swear my patience was wearing thin. There was no hug from my brother which was super strange. My husband was still just shocked.

"Where are my niece and nephew?" My brother finally said.

I explained they were with our parents. I needed a night out and I took it. Maybe next week I'll find a job. Complete crickets met my sarcasm. This had proven to be a hard crowd to please tonight. Interesting as that was, I just wanted to have a good time. I headed back to Khloe.

"Let's go. I know another place we can go."

She asked where I'd been and for some reason I lied and said the restroom. There was no push back or another word from my husband Lennox when I abruptly walked away. I expected them both to be excited to hang out with me for a change, but they just appeared surprised. It was a strange encounter to say the least.

Khloe was all set for the next stop although she didn't understand why I wanted to leave so abruptly. I was feeling a little depleted after my encounter in the club. I explained to Khloe that I had no desire to continue the night and instead would drop her off and head home. Alone time was sounding like exactly what I needed. Khloe had me drop her at a friend's house instead. I didn't mind; I just needed some time to reflect on the night's events.

When I returned home, everything just felt strange to me. I saw my husband and brother, and they treated me as an outsider rather than a part of their family. I was still baffled. Overall, I had minimal complaints, as Tron provided significant financial support for both the children and me. However, I often ask myself is that enough? He is bringing in tons of money, if I'm being honest He is bringing in more than I would think was possible unless he was seeing a patient every couple of minutes.

I know his father and Lennox are doing a lot to help, but I do hope it is all above board. His dad has had some issues in the past and Lennox lost his last job due to questionable behavior with insurance companies. I think I will pay them a visit soon. Maybe I will be welcomed or maybe it will go much like the bar incident. One thing I am certain of is, it is time for me to go back to work. As a doctor, starting my practice is my priority.

Chapter 11

Dr. Tron Ford

A few weeks had passed since Lennox and I slept together the first time. We had not tried to pause since. He was amazing in every way, and I am not sure I could let him go. I do know, however, being married to his sister is a huge problem. My dad walked in the office one day while we were getting a little close, but we recovered quickly. I am not sure we fooled him. My dad explained he was there to talk to me, and it needed to be in private.

He asked, "Aren't you done for the day? Why are you both still cooped up in this office?"

"I will be right with you, dad," I said. "Lennox before you go, I want to show you the insurance claims in my office."

Lennox accompanied me to my office.

"That was close," he said.

"We should probably exercise more caution in the future. Let me try to figure out what my dad wants to talk about. I will be by your house on my way home."

When I returned to my dad, he asked, "Is everything okay with you and Londyn?"

"Of course they are."

I think he was happy to hear that. He went on to explain he would have to stop helping in my practice. I thought that was strange since I was making us both so much money. I had a 100% success rate, partially because like father like son, if the man could not provide a baby for his mate, I did. No one had a failure. After all, I had learned so much about success from my dad. This is why my practice was sought out across this country. I barely had to advertise. My customers were advertising for me.

I had made sure my practice was airtight. I refused to end up like my dad. He barely escaped jail time. I could barely handle all the money I was taking in, and to increase the already risky practices, I had let Lennox teach me how to bill insurance companies in excess of what the procedures cost. I was bringing in so much money. I started to separate some out for myself and Lennox to have time alone.

Of course, being at his house was always risky. We finally decided to rent a condo for us, and if those walls could talk, that story would be hot. The sex was amazing, but he was starting to feel irritated when it was time for us to part for the night. He was always trying to get me to stay the night, sometimes I did. I told Londyn I fell asleep on the couch in my office.

The conversation with my dad was somber at best. He explained he had Lung Cancer that was in its final stages and doctors had told him if he lived three more weeks, that would be a miracle. The first thought that entered my head was my mom. There was an unbearable sadness that came over me. It is difficult to comprehend the possibility of losing both of my parents at such a young age. I expressed to my dad that he had to immediately start treatment and fight for his life. He politely declined and explained it was too late for him.

Three weeks later, my dad took his final breath in the presence of Londyn, and I felt much like a piece of me left with him. After the funeral was over, I was approached by my dad's lawyer. He explained, my dad wanted him to meet with me to go over his last will and testament. We made plans to do that. I was in no rush.

Honestly, I would rather prolong things as much as possible. I asked him if there would be anyone else there for the reading, and he explained that he asked that my wife and brother-in-law be present as well. That made sense, he knew I was the sole provider for my wife, and he had learned how close myself and Lennox were from working with us at my clinic.

My life was going through so many changes lately; I could hardly keep up. Londyn and I had been fighting a lot, although it had been paused since I lost my dad. She was so supportive and as always, a great wife. I noticed that her and Lennox also seemed to be taking a break. They barely talked at all. I wasn't 100% sure why, but if I had to guess, I would say a woman's intuition is a powerful thing. I really got married thinking I would be able to leave my thoughts and sex life with Zion behind, but I was not expecting a replacement so close by.

Lennox had fell into my life and I love every moment we spent together. The sex was amazing and really had me neglecting sex with my wife. It was one of the reasons why us fighting had become the norm. A week had passed since the funeral and Lennox, and I could not be any closer if we were married. I did not know how to fix the mess I made. I tried to pretend I wasn't gay, and Lennox was temporary the same as Zion. Sadly, I couldn't convince myself this was true. Lennox was the first thing I thought about every morning and the last person I thought about at night. I was even neglecting time with my kids. Londyn expressed how she felt like a single mom, and I couldn't even defend myself.

Chapter 12

Dr. Londyn Price

I had become a detective lately. If my husband paid me any attention at all, he would've realized the days he finally came home to spend time with the kids, I always had plans with Khloe. That could not be further from the truth. I was spending hours at his clinic going through his books, bank accounts, insurance claims, and patients. I thought it was a great idea to capture a picture of each child born successfully under his care. Some he even had a weird resemblance to. I didn't think anything of that, though.

So much time had to be spent with each couple and babies often looked like a ton of people at once. Looking at the insurance claims, I thought back to why Lennox had lost his last job after eight years. Some of the costs and billing at my husband's practice were just off. From inflated cost, to claims based on procedures that would not be administered in a fertility clinic. I was seeing it all. My husband was successful, there was no doubt about that, but he was also cheating insurance companies. I made copies to hold on to some of the proof. Something told me, I may need it later and both Tron and Lennox had their signatures all over this mess.

I paid a visit to Lennox's office as well. I was taken aback when I not only found lubrication but also condoms. Now when would that brother of mine find time to have his sexual tryst at work? I found the discovery strange. I had to ask myself, isn't Tron always in the office? Lennox is a mess and has become quite the quiet mess lately. He never called and even stopped returning my calls. I mentioned it to my parents, and they explained, they barely talked to him or saw him these days as well. They assumed he was just extremely busy working at the fertility clinic.

I was still stuck looking at the box of 24 condoms that barely had five left. I wonder who Lennox was seeing now? Maybe one day we will talk like old times, and I would ask. I also wanted to warn Lennox and Tron about the insurance fraud and give them a chance to discontinue what they were doing. I had made a mental note to pay them both a visit in the office. Hopefully, it will not be as awkward as when I ran into them at the bar. Either way, I need to protect my husband from himself because his choices affect the kids and me.

He did not have the liberty to drastically alter my life as his father had done to him and his mother before she passed away. I needed peace in my home and only God was welcome. The mass of paperwork and fraud in his office was not that of God's doing. He was breaking the law and his physician's oath. I could not be more disappointed in him. I would think he knew better. Soon we would be meeting with his dad's lawyer and something about that felt uneasy for me as well. I had told Tron it was a bad idea to have his dad helping him in the office and I still thought his influence had us here. Although, I also knew Lennox was surely not free of blame.

It was Friday night and according to Tron, he would be working late. Apparently, he had a couple coming from out of state and their plane had been delayed. As a courtesy he told them he would see them late in his office. I thought this would be the perfect time for me to head to his office and talk to him and Lennox. I dopped my kids off to my parents on the way. This had become a regular occurrence, and I was enjoying my time being kid free.

It gave me motivation to job hunt, have a night on the town with Khloe, and relax and reflect as well. It was 6:15 pm when I arrived at my husband's clinic. I had a nervous feeling in my stomach. I noticed Lennox was still there as well, but I didn't see any extra cars. This meant I had beat his patients' arrival as I had hoped. I walked in quickly as rain had begun to come down. The bell rang as always to alert a door had been opened. No one greeted me, however.

I was in the middle of the clinic when I started to hear Lennox's voice.

"Take that baby. Oh My God! I love being inside you."

Of course, my mouth was wide open. I thought to myself, I would soon know who my brother had been seeing, but for now I won't interrupt and would head to my husband's office. I was surprised he was nowhere to be found. The sex got louder between the two men as I walked to the lounge to check for Tron.

"Fuck me harder," I heard.

And the person I heard saying that sounded a little like Tron. But I knew that was my mind playing tricks on me. I mean that was impossible because I knew the first voice I heard was from Lennox. As I got closer to Lennox's office, my stomach was doing flips and I literally felt sick like I would throw up. I continued quickly down the hall. My impatience taking control of my feet.

I busted in Lennox's office and what I saw made me lose my balance. My husband was bent over in Lennox's chair and my brother was giving him every inch he had to give. Lennox noticed me first, yet he did not react at all. His face had the weirdest smirk as he continued to take my husband. Tron finally opened his eyes and there I stood. He immediately moved his body away from Lennox.

"Baby, please let me explain, it's not what it looks like."

"It's exactly what it looks like," I replied.

I turned on the heels of my shoes and left them both where they stood.

Chapter 13

Dr. Tron Ford

I was still trying to swallow, no pun intended, the events of yesterday. I could not believe my wife had walked in on me having sex with her bother. I was smart enough not to go home, but every time I tried to call, she would not pick up the phone either. To make matters worse, Lennox had been M.I.A. as well. He dressed in a hurry after his sister walked out and left without a word. That was my last time having any contact with him. As if I needed to dread this day more than I already did, I had all this to deal with as well. Today was the official reading of my father's Will. I didn't expect to see Londyn or Lennox, but they had been told to be there.

I walked into the office feeling sad and was immediately greeted by my father's attorney.

"Feel free to go in and have a seat. I am on my way to grab a water for Londyn and Lennox."

I felt like all the air left my body as I made my way to his conference room. I could not believe they had both showed up. How would I face Londyn? Hell, how would I face either of them? I walked in and quickly took my seat. There was complete silence in the room. Not one word was spoken.

The attorney came in the room with three water bottles and said, "Let's begin."

So, he did. It turned out my dad had left his estate to the three of us in an even split. That gesture truly confused me. He asked that both his estates be sold and the funds be distributed between us three along with all the insurance policies and all the cash and bank accounts. I was shocked, but I had no fight in me to care. I could not believe my dad was gone at a time when I needed him more than ever. I don't think I can face this alone.

Attorney Waylon

"I know this may be shocking to you all. Dr. Ford came to me with specific instructions. There is more I must share with you. What I have to say should bring you all some clarity."

"As you may know Dr. Ford senior was the fertility doctor for your mom and dad Londyn and Lennox. They saw him over five different procedures trying to become pregnant. No matter what your dad did to help, Mr. Price's sperm could not make a baby for Mrs. Price. Dr. Ford Senior eventually used his own sperm to impregnate your mom."

I watched both Lennox and Londyn's mouths drop, I continued.

"Yes, the late Dr. Ford Senior is the father of all three of you."

"Are you fucking kidding me?"

"I wish I was." I let out a heavy sigh then continued. "By the time he knew who you all were, you were already pregnant with your brother's child. He thought it would be better to just let it play out."

I didn't know what else to say to any of them. My job was done, and I must say I'm glad it's over.

Dr. Tron Ford

I could not believe my ears. I was even more shocked when Londyn yelled, "So you are fucking your brother and your sister?" The attorney turned red in the face.

2 years later…

Londyn left me and never looked back, and Lennox followed suit. Before Londyn left, she drained our bank accounts, including the inheritance from my dad. She blackmailed me letting me know, if I tried to pursue something legal to gain my fortune, she would make sure I ended up in jail. She sent me an envelope of kids from my practice she had DNA tested and even had a ton of documentation of my insurance fraud. She told me that my only option was to crawl up under a rock and die and I better do it silently.

I knew not to play with a woman scorned, so I did not. I didn't know how I would live going forward. Londyn even stipulated that I could not practice medicine any more or she would report all my wrongdoings. She had taken the kids, and I was not allowed to see them. I literally had nothing. I had to leave it all to stay out of jail.

This is an account of my financial journey from possessing millions to becoming homeless and currently residing in a makeshift shelter. Lennox never contacted me again, so I don't know what happened to him. I do know…

"THEY SAY KARMA IS A BITCH AND THEY WERE RIGHT"!!!!

The End!!

B. Jackson was born and raised in Detroit, B. Jackson grew up in a loving, resilient household led by her single mother. Now a longtime resident of Farmington Hills, she holds a Master's in Higher Education Leadership and has dedicated 25 years to supporting students and institutions.

Her greatest joys are her daughter, her loving husband, and the laughter shared with her close-knit family. A founding member and current treasurer of EyeCU Reading & Social Network, B. Jackson's love for books began in her preteens—sparked by a Donald Goines novel—and continues to thrive today.

She enjoys shopping, traveling, and discovering new places, all of which reflect her vibrant and joyful spirit.

Karma Remembers Everything

By

Rhena D. Holmes

I knew today was going to be different than any other day that I've had. First of all, my alarm didn't wake me, it was a lyric from a Tee Grizzley song that jumped me right into 'get yo' ass up mode'. It kept playing over and over in my head "*Being broke did something to my spirit.*" I had to get up to knock this last day of school out.

I have been a teacher for over thirty years, and I am contemplating my next move. I am ready to retire. Teachers are not respected like they were before and this new generation of students are not held accountable like they should be. I started in the late 90s in Inkster, MI and I thought I knew everything, I didn't. I will never forget when Madisyn's mom came and got me together.

I had no clue about grading, building relationships, communicating with parents, teacher evaluations, none of that. All I knew was that I wanted my students to like me and we were going to have big fun. Well, ShaSha, her mother, was not about that "bullshit I was teaching" (her words not mine). After she got me together about my dress, my lack of classroom management and communication, I knew that I had to change if I wanted to continue teaching. That one interaction created a friendship that lasted throughout my teaching career and personal growth into the woman I am today. ShaSha has stayed on my head and kept me calm on days when I thought I was losing it.

I woke up late and kept that Tee Grizzley song on repeat while I showered and dressed. I was packing my lunch when I heard the ding on my phone letting me know that I was receiving a text. It was my morning prayer from Ms. ShaSha. I responded with a heart and headed straight out the door. I got to my car and lo and behold that song was playing again; I knew right then that was a sign that today was going to be a crazy day. I turned the car over again wondering why it wasn't starting but the radio was playing. I looked over at the dashboard and saw my gas light was on. *"Being broke did something to my spirit"* blared through my speakers, all I could do was laugh.

Since it was the last day of school my principal knew it was going to be a day of shenanigans. She laughed at my predicament when I called and told her that I would be there by nine. I am usually there by 7:15 AM to support the breakfast crew and get the students to class, but it was field day, and the students were expected to show up with their families. So, I had time. As I waited for AAA to bring me some gas, I reflected on my years of teaching and interacting with students. I have had some laughs and cries over the years.

When I chose to be a teacher I did it for the benefit of having weekends and summers off, but that didn't happen. I coached and had games on weekends. In the summer, I eagerly signed up to teach summer school. In my reflection, I understood that helping people without voices was my calling, and teaching was my pathway to help.

Ding

The idea for my next career move just popped into my head. I will work in a shelter supporting those without voices, children that need help. And students who are aging out of foster care and need support. Whew, my mind was working overtime. I was excited about my next step. As I pulled into work, I got another ding from my book club, EyeCU Reading, reminding me that we had a meeting on Saturday and a photoshoot on Sunday. First thought, my weekend is shot. Second thought, I am retiring; I can celebrate all weekend with my book club.

When I thought about retiring my book club was the first to know. We always say that we are not your ordinary book club; we have been rocking strong for over 15 years. We have shared our life's highs and lows, and supported each other through personal and family challenges. We have become sisters (not by blood but relation). To surround myself with women who value my presence and hold me to a higher standard of womanhood was a goal while growing up, and these women have done just that. So, I knew after the photoshoot that celebrating us collectively as I got into retirement mode was the move. I called Ebony, our book club president, and asked her if she could use her connects at the comedy place in Southfield to book us a few seats for Sunday night. Once my plan was in my motion, my last school day was ready to begin.

I didn't tell anyone at the school that I was retiring except my principal, I had only been at the school for three years and I didn't want a fake celebration. I just wanted to disappear into the day and enjoy my new life of retirement. So, when the day was done, it was done.

Tam, the baby girl of EyeCU set up a wonderful photo shoot. Group shots, head shots, silly shots were all a part of the package but what I overlooked was the interview portion.

My whole teaching career, I was the teacher that knew everything about the students. I knew where they lived, who they lived with, and who their friends were, but I did not share many things about me. Even when we had the dreaded family tree project that I had to assign yearly to students, I only put me down and in the last ten years I put my sisters of EyeCU down as family. Now don't get me wrong, I have a mom and dad, but I have always felt that something was missing.

During the interview we were asked to share funny stories, how we developed a love of reading, our community involvement and anything book related. I was able to share how magazines like *Ebony Jr.* and *Jet* started my love for reading then I transitioned into novels in my teen years. My first experience with a love story as a teenager was titled *Ludell*, by Brenda Wilkinson. The story was set in the Deep South about a young lady who was given to her grandmother to raise because her mother was too busy chasing the American dream. After the interview was over, I stayed in a trance comparing Ludell's story to mine. We were total opposites, but I really connected with the character.

After the photoshoot was over, we headed to the comedy show in our full makeup and little black dresses. EyeCU was in the building, and we did not come to play. My club sisters Sam and Tina asked their brother, Shawn E, to open up the show with skits about teachers and students. I laughed until my cheeks couldn't take it anymore. We had laughter and joy on lock. I knew that I was going to enjoy retirement and have sisters to support me in my new transition. I waited until the end of the night to tell everyone that I would settle the bill. I pulled out my credit card and handed it to our waitress. As we were saying our goodbyes, Stacye waited with me. Stacye shared with me that there was a young lady in the crowd that shared similar features with me, as a writer she saw something new she would write about. She only had an idea and title "Doppelgänger" but she was ready. We chatted about the idea as we waited. When the waitress returned with my bill and credit card and I signed and slid my card into my purse. I said my final goodbyes and left.

Retirement in the summer has been such a good thing for me. I have just been living carefree, waking up when I want to, dating, bills on auto pay, and wine in the refrigerator. When I left education, I did not take a single thing with me but my memories. I was able to enjoy retirement so much better after I released the baggage of the system.

As I was sipping my special tea, I decided that I would take a spontaneous trip. I would pull out my credit card and book a luxury vacation on a coastal island. I wanted to go somewhere that I'd never explored, I had decided on the Maldives. I went to my secret stash and pulled out my credit card to pay. When I pulled out the card to pay the site needed my credit card verification code on the back. That's when I noticed a phone number in the signature space. I looked and stared at it. I had never noticed the phone number before and had not used my card since EyeCU took over the comedy club. Being very leery of scams, I cancelled the card and decided not to call the number back.

The last Saturday of the month is book club so before we talked about the book, I decided to share and gather the thoughts of my sisters on this phone number. It had been on my mind for three weeks. Once I told them about the mysterious number on the card, their minds went to work.

"What's the area code?" Bayyinah, the very focused one, asked.

"254."

"Do know anybody from Texas?"

"No."

I was bombarded with question after question that I didn't have the answer to. I decided to turn my phone on to record the conversation. Because like you would suspect what happens when nine women start talking, everyone is talking at once. At least with a recording, I could go back and try to catch everything. Maybe that way, I could come up with some answers.

While listening, I heard Monique in the background say,

"Have you told your parents?"

No. For what? I thought to myself.

Being retired left me with a lot of alone time. Time to contemplate my thought, my next move and replay conversations over in my head. The mystery of this phone number started to take over. But I decided to leave it alone and move on with my life.

Summer was over and a new school year was beginning; I decided that I would return to my former place of work and help parents with registration and teachers with last minute classroom setup. I was retired, not unmotivated. I love decorating and making my spaces bright and fun, a trait that I wanted to continue sharing with up-and-coming educators. Back in my element, I immediately requested to help out with registration and the parent teachers' association. Working with children in education had always had a place in my heart and being back just continued my love for helping the future generation. While there I also started an after-school care program to help single mothers. I loved being back in my element of helping others.

On my off days, I would exercise and read but the phone number on the back of my credit card still haunted me. No matter how much I tried to forget it, I would take it out every couple of days just to stare at it. Monique's question kept swirling in my head, so I told my mom and dad about the number. Their response was to make up dating jokes. They reasoned that it could have been from my prince charming.

While I love my parents, all they ever talked about was my choices in men and why didn't they have grandchildren. They were tired of the Cabbage Patch dolls as their grandchildren. I let them chide me every time we talked, but I saw how hard it was just to raise me, and I didn't want to take the chance of being a single mother. My mom always thought it was selfish of me not to have children; she was so old-fashioned. I always wanted to ask her if she loved children so much why did she only have one. But my father supported my decision. We always had long talks about how societal rules were changing and people felt independent and free in their choices. My dad is a great listener and supporter. It was then I decided to call the number on the back of the card.

As I got ready for my trip to the Maldives, I decided I would call from my layover flight and use a phone other than mine. While waiting to board my flight at Dubai International Airport, I used the amenities provided by the Oasis Pool Bar. I indulged in a hookah and made my first international call. I slowly dialed (254) 515-6350. My emotions of fear and anxiety were running rampant. I felt like I was making a huge mistake, then I felt like there was no turning back. No one answered, but there was a dial tone and a message that stated I have the answers to questions you need to ask. I listened and replayed the message over and over again before I boarded my flight to the Maldives. Once I landed, I was ferried to my hut at the Pullman Maldives all-inclusive resort. While there I planned to partake in the sun and relax, but I could not get the message that I heard off of my mind.

What did it mean?

Was it for me?

Is this a game?

After returning home, I called ShaSha to tell her what had transpired with the phone call. Per the usual we went out to J. Alexander's to talk.

"Well, what you gone do?"

That was the first thing out of ShaSha's mouth as soon as we were seated.

"I'm going to call again. I just need to make sure I heard what I thought I heard."

"Call now."

"I'll do it when I get home."

"No Bitch. Do it now. While you have me here," she insisted.

The phone only rang once.

"I knew you would call back," an elderly voice spoke to me through the phone's speaker.

I tried to gather my thoughts and my emotions to ask questions. Perhaps some of those questions that were asked in the meeting by my sisters. For the life of me, I couldn't think of one.

"I have the answers you are seeking," the voice said.

I had no idea what to ask but ShaSha did.

"Who this?" ShaSha asked.

"You aren't the one that should be asking questions," the voice responded then the call disconnected.

ShaSha was immediately angry, and I was too embarrassed to call back. The mood had definitely changed from jovial conversation to angry questioning. I had no idea how to proceed. We continued with the drinks and dinner while pouring over the mystery of the call. Once I got home, a replay of the phone call churned over and over in my head. I could not figure out where to begin. Again, I wanted to put it out of my mind.

I went back to my routine of working at the school parttime and planning my next vacation. On Wednesdays after work, I usually visit my parents' house, run errands and have dinner. Today was the day that I shared with them the mystery of the phone number. My parents sat and listened as I spoke, they waited until I finished to ask me a barrage of questions.

My mom asked me more direct questions like, why did I call, did I recognize the voice, did I hear anything in the background? Something about her line of questioning had gotten under my skin. She made me feel like I was wrong for being curious or that it was silly for me to think about. I was irritated with the situation and did not want to sit and listen to her questioning me.

My father, on the other hand, asked me questions that supported my emotions, how I felt, was I afraid, how could he help? He made me feel safe. I poured into him everything that I was feeling, all the questions I'd asked myself. My mom looked stone faced and emotional during our exchange.

I laid out my longing to feel like I belonged, that I wanted siblings. He listened to me rattle on about how I didn't have friends until I grew up and I felt like I was an outcast. I went as far back to when I first had to do the family tree assignment at Edison Elementary School. My teacher, Ms. Evans, teased me because I only had the three of us in the tree. I cried and told him how I wanted cousins and sleepovers. But I couldn't because I was their pride and joy, and they did not allow me to be around others.

My dad moved from his side of the table to console me and remind me of the sister/friends that I have made with my girls in EyeCU. I still was not satisfied. As I sat there thinking about all that I'd just said, I realized that I threw myself into my work. In all the years I worked, I had not poured into myself. It was time to pour into me, and I was at a point in my life where I was ready to do it.

I went home emotionally drained. My parents called to make sure I made it home, we chatted, and I drifted off into an uneasy slumber. Sleeping did not help ease my troubles; my mind was not at ease. I tossed and turned all night. I couldn't stop thinking about my mother's stern, tight-lipped expression.

My alarm went off for "work" the next day and I couldn't even get up to turn it off. My body was tired, my spirit felt broken. I was in a funk, and I felt it. Suddenly, a breeze flew across me and startled the laziness out of me.

I got up with the quickness turned the alarm off, hopped in the shower, made my bed and did two loads of laundry. I had the energy of a toddler running with the remote when everyone is watching TV. I could not explain where this burst of energy came from. It took me a minute to make the connection. It was restlessness and uncertainty that had come from the day before that could only be fixed with a phone call.

I knew that I needed to make that call to ease my mind, this time I wanted to be prepared. I didn't know how to start the conversation, what to say, when to call or how to feel. I just knew in order to crush these feelings that I had I needed to make that call. I wanted to call Sha Sha and get some pointers, but I knew that this was a task that I had to complete on my own. So, I pulled up that recording and wrote down some questions.

It was the last Saturday of the month, time for my book club meeting. I RSVP'd weeks ahead of time that I would not be attending. I knew what had to be done and that day. I knew when all of the sister friends were meeting they would hold me in prayer to support my absence and journey into the unknown. During the day I psyched myself up with a visit to Damn Momma's Edibles and Eateries. I ate the edible, and I knew it was time.

As soon as I heard the voice my questions came flowing but I couldn't find my voice. I was excited and fearful at the same time. I was scared of what would become, afraid of how my life would change once I started asking questions.

"Who are you?"

"I am the answer." *What kinda cryptic shit is this?*

"Well, what do you want?"

"I want you to know who you are and your beginnings."

"Are you gone tell me or not?!" I spat with full irritation.

That's when the truth was told.

"My name is Antonia West," she hesitated. "I'm your grandmother," she stated.

As soon as I heard those words, I hung up.

I had way more questions than answers. If that were true, the only people that could give me answers were my parents. I went straight to their house, forgetting that I had taken an edible. When I got to my parents' house, I was looking and feeling high as hell. My mind was in a fog.

"Which one of you lied about me having a grandmother?"

That's the last thing I remember screaming at them before I woke up in a daze on the couch, I'm assuming I passed out on. My mother's eyes bore down on me with a helluva glare. I saw it as a stern warning, "Don't go stirring up shit!"

After a cup of coffee, I sat down at the kitchen table with my parents telling them about the previous day's events. I was in serious thought trying to figure out which one of my parents lied to me and why. And I suppose the answer to my question is both of them lied. My whole life, I thought it was just the three of us. But they refused to acknowledge me, the question or my feelings and we just sat there looking at each other. After too many moments of neither of them saying a word, I took that as my cue to leave.

It seemed the only person willing to give me answers was the stranger on the phone. So, I called the number... well, my grandmother back.

"Do you have a son or a daughter?"

I wasn't fully invested in what she was saying but I didn't want to give her any answers if this was some kind of scam. You know, like the fortune tellers that just tell you what you want to hear after you've given them a little information.

"I had twins, a boy and a girl."

"What are you telling me?"

"It's been so long since I've seen them. I just want to know you. Know if they were safe."

She couldn't be saying what I think she's saying. This woman is not trying to tell me that my mother was my aunt, and my father was my uncle. *What in the entire fuck has happened to my life.*

I sat on the phone outdone and flabbergasted as I listened to her recount of things that happened before I was born. She shared how my parents fled to Michigan to get away from the stares, the ridicule.

"No matter how much I beat 'em, tried to keep them apart, they shared a passion that just couldn't be broken."

The realization of her words made me sick to my stomach. I was now wishing I'd never dialed that number. I didn't even care to know how she knew who I was or even how she got the number on my card in the first place. Some things should be left unsaid. The very secret that my parents hid from has turned my world into the ultimate clusterfuck.

A whirlwind of thoughts hit me all at once. Now I know why I never had branches on my family tree nor had siblings. They couldn't legally be married, could they? They got lucky with me not having any defects. Isn't that what they say about those kinds of kids? Hell, I am one of those kids. Is that why they didn't have any more? Did they think I'd be like them? Did they feel like more kids would bring them their karma?

"Are they happy?"

Antonia's question jarred me from my thoughts. She'd been talking but I wasn't listening. Somehow, that question brought me back to reality.

"What?!" I questioned, with a bit of indignation.

"I'm not long for this world. I just want to know if they're happy."

I didn't know how to answer her. What was I supposed to say? Yes. Your children are living happily ever after as sister/brother/husband and wife?

"I guess."

That was the only answer I could muster. I was trying to figure out how I could look at them without vomiting. I was thinking of how I would address them. Would I even talk to them again? If they were happy was nowhere on the spectrum of things I cared about right now.

"I know this might be too much for you. But, like I said, I ain't too long for this world."

She went on to say that she was sorry for telling me like this, and sorry she couldn't do anything, sorry she hadn't found me sooner in life, sorry she disrupted my life. Then she followed all those apologies with a 'but'.

"But you have the right to know. And like I always told my twins, what's done in the dark, will always come to light."

Rhena D. Holmes is a proud twin and first-time author whose passion for storytelling was inspired by her parents, Alvin and Delores Holmes. With decades of experience in education, Rhena is deeply committed to promoting literacy among children and nurturing a love for reading from an early age. Her debut in Karma is a testament to her dedication to lifelong learning and creative growth.

Ain't No Fun When the Rabbit Has the Gun

By

M.L. Hawkes

Chapter 1

Derek had a great feeling about the interview. The phone call to schedule the interview showed promise as Derek had been out of work for close to a year and he was beginning to wonder if anyone would hire him. Derek's savings were dwindling, and his unemployment check for $362/week was chump change compared to the $137,000 salary he pulled in prior years.

Jess, his college sweetheart, was now his wife and mother of his two kids. Jess was a stay-at-home mother who enjoyed interacting with other moms while their kids had swim lessons, gymnastics, or story time at the local library, all while the moms sipped on their elaborate coffee drinks and gossiped about the comings and goings in their small town. Derek and Jess led a comfortable and effortless existence until budget cuts and a business merger caused Derek to be on the unfortunate side of the unemployment line.

Derek worked his way up the corporate ladder, starting out as a delivery driver, lead driver, supervisor and ultimately Logistics Manager for Medquest Home and Medical Supply. Derek had a business degree, and while he didn't possess a post baccalaureate education, Derek was savvy enough to use charm, charisma and white privilege to secure his place in middle management.

Derek had grown accustomed to being in charge, ruling his drivers with a stern fist, especially the minority employees. He possessed a disdain for brown and black drivers. Derek's hypocrisy ran deep and was clear to even a blind man that Derek treated black drivers differently. Derek didn't try to hide his favoritism, and he was bold with it, daring anyone to question his judgment. He favored the drivers that looked like him and he was skeptical of those that didn't.

He treated black drivers like a necessary evil. Derek gave the black drivers the hardest assignments, their deliveries were made to high rise apartments in the inner city where there was a high probability the elevators were out of order. The white drivers were afforded the desirable shifts, suburban locations and better vehicles. White drivers had cushy assignments to luxury condominiums and senior convalescent homes that were a step below a country club.

Anastasia, Stacye for short, worked in Human Resources. Stacye was cool with everybody at Medquest Home and Medical Supply. She was the person you wanted on your side because she made things happen; she made a great ally. Michelle and Melissa were both patient care representatives who interacted with patients, scheduling their home deliveries and orders for medical supplies. Monica was a home care nurse who provided skilled nursing care to patients in their home. Stacye and the Three Musketeers as they were affectionally called, went to lunch, hung out outside of work and were in a book club together. They were more than colleagues they were good friends.

One day, over lunch, Stacye, Michelle, Melissa and Monica were having lunch in the breakroom, while the local news played in the background, idle chit chat occurred as the ladies discussed their weekend. Stacye said she had a chill weekend as she hung out with her mom, did a little shopping, took the dogs to the groomer, went out with a prospective date that turned out to be a dud.

"Aww, Stacye, another dud?" Michelle questioned. "I have someone you might be interested in."

"No thanks, I know your taste in men, and I would rather be alone."

Michelle rolled her eyes in disgust and proceeded to tell everyone about her weekend. Melissa let them know she worked on Saturday, but it was pretty quiet in the office, so she read Hwy 725 by Kaylynn Hunt and Octavia Grant to pass the time.

Monica told everyone that she heard from an old friend that she used to work with back in the day who was looking for a new job.

"I hope he isn't a nurse because there aren't any openings here, but we do have a couple CNA openings available," Stacye stated.

"He was a driver at the old place," Monica informed.

"We have an opening in dispatch for a driver, but he would have to work under Derek,"

"That asshole," Monica whispered. "I would rather be unemployed than work under that slick motherfucker. Y'all see how he treats the minority drivers compared to the white drivers. Tell me, Stacye, how does he get away with it?"

Stacye shrugged.

"Unfortunately, the minority drivers give them a reason to be fired. Timecard fraud, theft, waste and repeatedly being late and call ins. Derek uses all that to justify his actions. That's not to say the others don't do it. He just focuses on the minorities. You know we have to be ten times better and work ten times harder."

"And still must keep our nose clean just to keep a job than our white counterparts do with the minimum effort," Michelle added.

"That's some bullshit," Melissa said. "I see some of the white drivers doing things and Derek just looks away. One day, Derek will get his. Karma will be on that ass!"

On that note ladies, we need to get back to work before we lose our jobs," Monica joked.

Monica sat at her desk and thought it might not be a good idea to have her friend, Jermaine, work at Medquest under Derek. Jermaine was a good colleague and provided excellent care and service to patients. While Medquest provided great benefits and compensation, the way the drivers were treated was questionable. She had to give serious consideration to Jermaine's request for a job. Monica would feel horrible if things didn't work out as Jermaine was a single dad with kids to provide for. As Monica pondered, she decided to call Jermaine and share her concerns about the job with him.

Jermaine answered after one ring.

"What's up, Monica?"

"Nothing much. I was thinking about our conversation and called to share my thoughts on your interest in working at Medquest. You see, your potential boss, how can I say this? He's a racist asshole! He treats the minority drivers differently than the white drivers. I don't want to subject you to that type of mess, and everything ends up going south," Monica vented.

"Listen Monica, I can handle my own, just let me know if I can list you as a reference."

"You can list me as a professional reference, but if things don't work out, don't say I didn't warn you."

"Bet! Remember that I'm a praying man. What do I always tell you?"

Monica repeated the phrase the Jermaine often used, "If you're going to pray, don't worry."

"So don't worry about me, they will love me, and you know I will do a good job."

Monica chuckled as she sent Jermaine the job link so he could apply online.

"Good luck. Talk to you soon," she said before disconnecting.

Monica walked to Stacye's office to give her a heads up about Jermaine applying.

"Hey girl", Monica said, poking her head into Stacye's office.

"Come on in. Shut the door."

"What's up?" Monica questioned as she did as requested.

"You won't believe the shit I have to deal with around here. I must mediate a disciplinary meeting between Jessica and Sabrina in accounting because Jessica felt it necessary to tell Sabrina that black people don't wash their hair every day. Sabrina snapped back saying, *we might not wash our hair every day, but we do wash our ass every day!*" Stacye and Monica shared a laugh at the statement. "Now Sabrina done filed a grievance against Jessica."

"I'm surprised that Sabrina handled the situation so well," said Monica.

"Sabrina is smart and no one is going to mess up her bag. You know she and Jessica are going for the Service Lead position in accounting? It is almost guaranteed to go to Sabrina now," Stacye informed her.

"I almost forgot the reason why I came in here. Jermaine still wants to apply even though I told him my concerns about Derek. So, when you see his name put in a good word with Derek. I know how much he listens to you—well the way he looks at your ass."

"Girl please. I'm not thinking about Derek's ass, and I know he would like some of this good-good, but he can keep his thirsty ass looking. Because he could never with me!" Stacye said.

"Ok girl, I have patients to see, I will talk to you later."

Chapter 2

Jermaine started working with Medquest Home and Medical Supply and everything was going well until it wasn't. Jermaine worked at Medquest for close to a year and a half. Jermaine was a hard worker, dependable, well liked and appeared to get along with patients and staff. Jermaine's supervisor received many compliments from patients praising him for the excellent service he provided.

One morning, Stacye was talking to Jermaine in the breakroom when Derek entered. Derek listened as Stacye and Jermaine talked about how great the Maxwell concert they attended over the weekend was. Derek wondered why Jermaine would be with Stacye outside of work. *Were they a couple?* Derek was pinged with jealousy. Little did Derek know that Stacye, The Three Musketeers and a couple of other drivers attended the concert together as a group.

"It's about time to get on the road isn't it, Jermaine? It's company time," Derek called out across the room.

***

Derek had a secret desire for black women. That is Something no one would ever know. It was a hunger that he wished he could satisfy but for now he would have to settle for fantasizing while making love to Jess. If Jess knew how much he yearned and thought about his colleagues, the girl at the coffee shop or the sexy neighbor jogging past his house in the evening with a voluptuous ass that bounced as she waved when she ran by, she would be livid. For now, Derek could only wonder saying, "Hi, Ms. Faulkner" as that ass bounced away.

While Jess was a beautiful woman even after two kids, she still turned heads when she was out alone or with her girlfriends, but she lacked a sufficient derriere, something that Derek wished he could have if only for one time. Jess and her lack of ass left Derek imagining what it would be like to be with a black woman. When Derek was making love to Jess, he would envision Anastasia. Derek always wanted to grab a hold of all her ass from behind while thrusting his dick inside of her juicy, wet pussy. What was the saying, the darker the berry the sweeter the juice? Derek wanted all the nectar.

Thinking of what Jermaine could've been doing with Stacye stoked the fire of jealousy sitting at the base of his spine. Derek was often seen in Stacye's office. Most thought it was because of Derek's track record with the drivers. But Stacye had ass for days and her professional, yet seductive personality piqued Derek's interest from the moment they met. She was always cordial and pleasant But she never smiled at him the way she had Jermaine. It was almost as if she avoided him when Jermaine was around.

***

Not long after, Derek saw Jermaine cozy with Stacye, Jermaine received a verbal warning for lack of efficiency and productivity for his delivery times. He was shocked.

Drivers were allocated a certain number of minutes to complete deliveries depending on the task performed. According to Derek, Jermaine spent more time making his deliveries to patients, compared to his peers. Jermaine explained that he talks to patients, helps them out and even prays with them. When Derek heard Jermaine's explanation for his lack of efficiency, he was livid.

"Your job is to deliver supplies and set up medical equipment such as oxygen, beds, commodes, not to minister to patients on Medquest time," Derek spat out.

To ensure he was complying, Jermaine began to adhere to Medquest's protocols. He made sure to adhere to the times allocated for delivery. Jermaine thought that would be sufficient until he was called into Derek's office yet again. This time he received a written warning for lack of efficiency and productivity for one of his stops from a couple weeks prior. Jermaine had exceeded that delivery by eighteen minutes.

"You had six oxygen cylinders and a case of diapers to deliver. What was the reason for the extended time at this location?" Derek inquired.

"Mrs. Johnson wasn't doing well spiritually and was lonely. I just sat and talked to her for a little bit to lift her spirits. Good customer service is about more than money and schedules."

"We'll see if you still feel that way if you don't have a job. Your next write up will be your final warning!"

Jermaine was fed up. He knew he was a good employee. Why was Derek singling him out after all this time?

As Jermaine was loading his truck for the day's deliveries, Stacye was walking from her car to enter the building. Stacye and Jermaine exchanged pleasantries. He stopped loading to speak with her.

"You know I was written up again," Jermaine informed. "This time, I took too long on a delivery because I was talking to lonely Mrs. Johnson."

"Derek nitpicks. Technically, there's nothing I can do. He uses policies to his advantage. Just do things exactly as protocol states."

"I think he's trying to fire me. But why now? After nearly two years, I thought it was all good. I need my job to provide for me and my family."

"Stick to the book, you'll be fine."

"Thanks for listening," Jermaine stated with gratitude.

Just as he turned to go back to finish loading, he noticed Derek watching from the window of the breakroom.

Later that night….

"What's up, Jermaine, everything ok?" Monica questioned once Jermaine picked up the phone.

"No, everything is not ok," Jermaine shouted.

He caught Monica up on everything that had been happening from the verbal and written warnings and letting her know that his next written warning will be the final warning, and he would be terminated.

"Wow," Monica said.

She felt awful that Jermaine was going through this with Derek, but she told him about Derek before he started working at Medquest.

"Do you know why Derek is singling me out and treating me this way?"

"All I know is that Derek is an asshole that I can't stand, and I keep our interactions to a minimum. Jermaine, all I can suggest is that you keep your head on a swivel, do your job, and cover your ass. Also, I would probably look for another job."

"Yeah, I think you are right, Monica. Maybe it is time for me to look at other options."

"That's right. This job isn't the end all be all. Let me know if you need another reference. You know, I got you!"

A couple weeks later, Jermaine was loading his delivery truck, Derek asked him to come to his office.

Again? What could he want with me this time?

Jermaine could see that he was the top driver meeting productivity goals according to the weekly metrics displayed on the dispatcher's bulletin board. He couldn't possibly be trying to come for his performance, AGAIN!

"I'm going to have to let you go," Derek said with a smug look on his face. "It's come to our attention that your driver's license is suspended."

"What?" Jermaine was completely caught off guard. "My license isn't suspended."

Derek threw a printout of Jermaine's Motor Vehicle Record at him, and it displayed his driving history, traffic violations and license status. SUSPENDED was listed as Jermaine's current license status. Jermaine couldn't understand it.

"I'm losing my job over an unpaid parking ticket that I wasn't aware of?" questioned Jermaine.

Jermaine pleaded as he stated that he had a family to provide for. Derek was not moved or concerned about

Jermaine's plight and proceeded to tell Jermaine to give him the company pager, cellphone, truck keys and to clear out his locker.

Jermaine called Monica from his car as he left Medquest for the last time.

"Well, they got me," said Jermaine.

"Who got you?" questioned Monica.

"Derek's punk ass fired me because my driver's license was suspended over an unpaid parking ticket that I was unaware of."

"What? I've known that to happen to other drivers and nurses and they allow you to correct problem and not be fired. But it is normally up to the manager's discretion. I'm sorry this happened to you, Jermaine."

"This is why I didn't want you to work under Derek."

"It's ok. I appreciate the opportunity you gave me. You tried to warn me."

They both said they would keep in touch, and their call concluded.

Monica marched into Derek's office after the call from Jermaine. She was on fire.

"What's up, Derek? I heard you fired Jermaine over an unpaid parking ticket."

"Yeah, it was unfortunate, as I really liked Jermaine, but I received his Motor Vehicle Record from Human Resources. My hands were tied."

"Your hands were tied?" You know, Derek, this has happened to other staff that drive company vehicles in the past and they weren't immediately fired. They were allowed to rectify the situation without dismissal."

"Like I said, my hands were tied."

"You'll reap what you sow, and I hope I'm there to witness it," Monica said before turning and marching out of Derek's office.

Stacye was on vacation, so she wasn't in the office to vent to. Instead, Monica went to talk to Michelle and Melissa.

"Dang, that's messed up," cried Melissa after Monica told them what happened.

"I'm sorry that happened to Jermaine," Michelle said.

"He's a good brother, preachy, but a good brother. I feel so guilty," Monica admitted.

"I can understand you feeling that way, Monica, but you shared your concerns with Jermaine, and he still made the decision to come and work at Medquest under Derek's punk ass," Melissa countered.

Chapter 3

Derek sat daydreaming about Anastasia. She was still heavily on his mind. But now, none of the time he'd spent with her mattered. The company merger had him on the outside while Stacye with her education and vast amount of experience landed as head of human resources. Derek sat deep in thought, trying to figure out how he could've done things differently when his cell phone rang.

"Hello, this is Rebecca, administrative assistant to the Director of Operations at BioGenomics Laboratories. We received your application for interest in the divisional logistics manager position and would like to schedule an interview if you're available."

Derek clenched his fist in a celebratory manner.

"It would be a pleasure. I'm available anytime."

***

Derek thought about the beautiful woman that sat across from him conducting the interview. Evette was her name. She came across as poised, articulate and confident in her role as Director of Operations. Evette appeared to be highly professional, firm and no nonsense as she described the details of Derek's potential role as Logistics Divisional Manager. It would be a demanding job overseeing not only the location in Michigan but locations in five other states. He would also be interacting with headquarters which was in another country.

Derek thought about the responsibility, and he was confident he could step up to the challenge. But could he report to a black woman as his boss? He had never reported to someone black, and it didn't sit well that he would have to start now. Evette was beautiful, like Stacye. If she had an ass like Stacye's, it would make that pill a bit easier to swallow.

But his options were nil, and this job would be the highest paying job he ever had. He didn't have many options. The job included travel, bonuses and other perks he was not accustomed to receiving. It checked all the boxes of his dream job. Internally, he was celebrating knowing his life would be better than ever with this new position.

Reporting to someone Black couldn't be so bad.

As the interview continued, Evette relaxed a little and even joked about some of the antics and quirks of the staff that worked at BGL.

"You hear everyone refer to the company as BGL. Much easier to say," Evette informed.

The arbitrary statement had Derek tingling on the inside. She was already referencing him working for the company.

I got this in the bag.

Evette gave Derek a tour of the building and showed him his potential office that overlooked the city. Evette had shared that BGL was a company that compensated their employees well and if hired, he would be impressed with BGL's compensation package. Derek couldn't wait to tell Jess that he not only had a job but a dream job that would take their lives to higher places.

As the tour concluded, Evette and Derek returned to Evette's office and continued to talk about the details of the role of Logistics Divisional Manager and Evette answered all of Derek's questions about the job. Evette looked at his resume to make sure she hadn't missed anything.

Derek saw visions of new cars, a new house, and traveling in his head knowing this job would be just what they needed. Maybe he'd even buy Jess an ass.

"Oh, I see, you worked at Medquest Home and Medical Supply? My sister is a nurse and used to work for that company, you might have known her."

Derek had a sudden look of concern, defeat and fright as his charismatic smile and his smug confidence disappeared from his face replaced with a deep crimson.

"I bet I know who your sister is. Now that you mention it, I see the resemblance. Monica, right?"

"Yes," Evette responded excitedly with a huge smile on her face.

All the visions in Derek's head suddenly melted away.

M. L. Hawkes, originally from Petersburg, VA, relocated to Detroit, MI as a young child. An avid reader since elementary school, she devoured everything she could get her hands on—from library books to the daily newspaper, including local news, lifestyle sections, sports, classifieds, and even the obituaries. A true book nerd, she has a deep love for mysteries, autobiographies, and a good love story.

As a founding member of the EyeCU Reading & Social Network, M. L. Hawkes is stepping out of her comfort zone by putting pen to paper with her inaugural short story in Karma. A devoted wife and mother, she also enjoys cooking, baking, playing games, and spending quality time with her family and friends.

Coming to the Stage: Karma

By

Tam Telling Tales

Hey guys. I'm Tina and these are my confessions of an Entreprenigga running my own business. My own sexual therapy business; for people with disabilities. To be honest, it was a great gig initially. I was a certified "intimacy coach". There weren't many of us around, so business was always plentiful. Most clients would want conversation, hugs, or a massage every now and then.

But, somewhere along the line the clients and their demands started to change. Soon, I found myself having to "use sexier voices" when I talked, or "run my finger down the small of a back" when I'm giving hugs. Considering it was sexual therapy; I figured it was justified. Clients would pay more for the extras, so I just did it. But things took a turn for the worse about 6 months ago when I met Jaime.

Jaime had quadriplegia. On a Wednesday morning, Jaime rolled into my office. He'd heard of me through another client (word of mouth was my best marketing tool). He asked to make an appointment for the upcoming Saturday. I told him I was booked and stayed pretty booked on Saturdays. After requesting Sunday and being told that I don't work on Sundays, Jaime pulled out a large wad of cash and requested that I reconsider taking him as a client on Sunday. I grabbed the cash, tucked it in my bra, and booked him for Sunday at 2PM.

I arrived 5 minutes early to Jaime's house and waited in the car until exactly 2PM. I walked up the stairs to the front door. I text Jaime, telling him that I had arrived. A minute later, he opened the door for me. He smelled like Sean John cologne and was dressed in a Polo jogging outfit. I love Sean John and I love Polo. Not bad for a guy I can't look directly in the face for longer than 2.7 seconds. As I entered, I noticed that he kept a neat and clean house. He must have very reliable care givers I thought to myself. We began chatting about nothing and laughing about everything. He told me about how he ended up in the wheelchair. He'd been racing on a 4x4, hit a pothole, flipped his bike over, and crushed several bones in his body. After disengaging from his bike during the accident, he hit the ground face-first and slid approximately 8 feet along the gravel. Needless to say, it left his face extremely distorted.

He was still of sound mind but wasn't the easiest guy to look at. His vocal cords were damaged during the accident as well, so his speech has a waspy sound. As the visit continued, I began to engage in my basic sexually stimulating techniques. Body rubs, earlobe blowing, you know, basic stuff. Once I began to massage Jaime's shoulders, I leaned down closer to him so that the back of his head could lightly lay upon my breasts. He moaned and I thought I saw a bulge in his lower region. I realized I was mistaken as I saw him remove his cell phone from between his legs. It had shifted from his lap as the therapy had begun. After approximately 30 minutes of therapy, we were done with our session, and I asked if he'd like to book his next appointment. He asked for my very next opening. The way he paid top dollar, I booked him for Tuesday and made a mental note to reschedule two of my appointments I already had.

Weeks went by and Jaime had become my best customer, I mean, patient. Although the therapy activities he'd request were untraditional as hell, and what some might even call humiliating, he was paying me cash and those trips to the bank to make deposits felt real good.

One Tuesday morning, I got a text from Jaime asking if he can come into my office instead of meeting at his home. I agreed. He also asks if he'd be allowed to bring in an outfit for me to wear. I agreed to that too. He arrived 10 minutes early for his appointment. He handed me the outfit and then retreated to the back lounge area where I conducted in-house therapy. Opening the bag, I noticed that Jaime had brought me a brown body stocking, leash & collar, and doggy ear headband.

"Oh, his ass trippin' today" I thought to myself.

I put the body stocking on but decided against the other items. I ain't nobody's Bitch. I walked into the lounge and sitting on the coffee table was a stack of money twice the size of the last one he gave me. So, I placed the headband atop my sew-in and asked for assistance in getting the collar around my neck. What can I say, I like money.

Similar to our other sessions, we began chatting and laughing. After getting myself warmed up, I began rubbing his legs and blowing on his earlobe. Before his massage began, he grabbed the leash that was dangling from my neck. "Sit," he demanded. Initially taken aback, I stood looking at him like he was crazy, but I quickly shook it off remembering that I was clearly wearing a collar and leash for a reason.

"Alright, here we go." I thought.

I sat Indian style on the floor in front of Jaime. He requested that I 'sit like a dog' on the side of him. I obliged him.

"Good girl" he responded.

He began petting my head. He kept instructing me on the different things he wanted me to do.

"Scratch behind your ear."

"Chase your tail."

Just a bunch of requests. Nothing sexual, but it was definitely arousing him. This time, I was sure he had a bulge, and it wasn't no phone. Then he asked me to let the sides of his wheelchair down and hump on him. If I had known my day was going to turn out like this, I'd have had some brown liquor and ate an edible. I let the sides down, straddled his lap and bounced up and down. With every downward motion, that bulge hit my thigh. Then, he says,

"I want you to hump on me. On my leg. Hump on my leg and breathe hard. Like a dog."

"On your legggggg?" I asked.

Jaime gives me this demanding grimace. I rise off his lap and position myself on the floor with his left leg between my thighs. I then began humping this man's leg. And when I looked between his legs again, I thought his manhood was goin' to bust out those jogging pants.

"Hump harder" he commanded.

I thrusted my pelvis further and harder into the side of his leg. So hard that I accidentally removed the break off the wheelchair. Simultaneously, Jaime was pressing his hand along the operational buttons on his arm handle. All of a sudden, his chair took off full speed ahead. I was stuck onto the chair since my body stocking got caught in the gears. We didn't stop until we both slammed into the exposed brick wall 50 ft away. The impact was hard, and I was stuck under the wheelchair and this big ol' freak nasty bastard. I couldn't move and apparently Jaime had been knocked out cold.

His cell phone was lying in arm's reach—screen cracked but functional. I called 911. I really didn't want to, but I legit couldn't move. My pride was going to have to take a back seat. The first responders had the nerve to snicker at me after they had got Jaime on the stretcher. That damn body stocking had gotten so tangled that they had to cut it off me so I could get off the floor. Now I'm standing there naked, with a dog collar, leash and dog ears on. The tallest first responder asked,

"Don't you dance at Ace of Spades?"

The shorter one embarrassingly elbowed him in the side.

"I USED to. I'm a therapist now."

"Therapistttttttt?" the taller one said.

"Dawg, would you chill?" the shorter one asked.

"I recognized you and your homeboy from the club, dat's all. I do security there sometimes when my cousin can't make it. The other girls were telling us that you were in the medical field now. So, dis your medical field?" tall responder asked jokingly.

"He not from the club. He's my therapy client" I responded coldly.

"Ok. That's cool what you doing for the homie now considering his situation. That accident jacked his face up."

"Wait. What? You really know him from the club?" I asked.

"Yeah, and you do too. This dat nigga Big J. He stayed trickin' on you. Dang girl. You act like you don't remember nobody. Bougie ass."

Still confused, I began to recollect the guy we all called Big J. He was fine and he loved for me to dance for him. He paid VERY well and was head over heels for me. Man, how could I forget that unforgettable night at the Velvet Rope. Looking over at Jaime, I soon realized he was Big J. The man who would always bark in my ear when I gave him lap dances. The man who had caused such a commotion at the club. He always smelled good and dressed nice in Polo gear. Yup, Jaime was definitely Big J. I couldn't tell because his beautiful face had been destroyed. He must have found out about me from one of the girls still at the club.

I wrapped myself in a robe and ran outside to catch up with the first responders before they pulled off.

"What happens now? Shouldn't you guys be taking his wheelchair?" I asked.

Short Responder says, "I thought that was yours."

Tall Responder had a bewildered look on his face.

"Why would the wheelchair be mine? He's the one that can't walk."

Now both of the responders were giving me a bewildered look.

"How you figure that Baby Girl? J might have a trash looking face now, but dat's about it. He walks his ass in the club just fine. This past Sunday as a matter of fact."

And now it's my turn to look bewildered. I stood there and tall responder finally broke the silence with a loud, hearty laugh.

"You thought this nigga couldn't walk? He Gypsy Rosed yo' ass!"

All the red flags started pouring into my brain: no wheelchair ramp at the house, grabbing the leash, petting my head while I was being a dog, GETTING HARD!!! Hell, the nigga literally opened the door at his house on the very first visit! He said he was a whole ass quadriplegic. How didn't I see it? All that damn money, that's how. I done let this man pay me to be stupid. I jumped on the back of the ambulance and leaned close to Big J's face. He was slightly conscious at this point.

"Why would you do this?" I began asking. "What satisfaction could you possibly get from this? You're sick!"

Big J had his eyes fully opened at this point and was looking me in the face when he responded, "Arf, arf!"

Tina blinked at Jaime, the pieces finally snapping into place like a bad puzzle she never wanted to solve.

Of course.

That night at the Velvet Rope.

One year earlier….

Look. I've seen a lot in this job. I've seen dudes cry during lap dances, get emotional when I play '90s R&B, and one man asked me to bless his chicken nuggets before eating them. But Big J? He was different.

He wasn't weird. He wasn't rude. He smelled good — always had on that Sean John like he bathed in it and then prayed over it. Walked in every Friday night like he owned stock in the place. Clean Polo fit; kicks always crisp.

He didn't get sloppy drunk like some of these dudes. He came in, got his usual drink — Henny, straight — found his seat (third from the stage, but not right up front, so you knew he had manners), and tipped respectfully. Never tried to cop a feel. Never said anything wild. But always barked in my ear before he paid.

So, when I saw him pull out a chain with a little heart charm on it Friday night, I thought he was returning a lost & found item.

He waved me over after my set.

"Tina," he said, low and cool, like the beginning of an R&B interlude. "Can I talk to you for a second?"

I leaned in.

"You good, J?"

He handed me the chain.

"I got this for you. It ain't nothin' crazy. Just... I wanted you to know I see you."

I blinked.

"Oh... okay. That's sweet."

Then he hit me with it.

"I was thinking... maybe you and me could get to know each other outside of this. Like, dinner. Not wings-at-the-bar dinner. Like real dinner. Date dinner."

Now I ain't gonna lie — for a half-second, my brain flickered. I imagined him in a hoodie, on a couch, watching *In the Heat of the* Night reruns handing me a plate of food he didn't cook but ordered with intention.

But then I remembered where I was standing. I had a thigh-high boot full of glitter, a club light in my left contact, and three songs left before my break. And every eye in the club was now on me.

The DJ, Petty Pete, had already sensed drama and killed the music like a vulture. The crowd was quiet — the kind of quiet that happens before a bar fight or somebody's mama shows up yelling.

I smiled. Professional. Calm. Dignified. But I leaned close and whispered:

"J… you fine, you cool, and you got cologne that actually lasts. But this ain't the Love & Hip Hop reunion. This the Velvet Robe, baby."

He chuckled, but he looked serious.

"I know what it is. I just figured… maybe you might wanna try something real."

I bit my lip.

"J, I am real. But in here, I'm also Tina — and Tina got a mortgage due, acrylic nails to fill, and a new business to open soon."

He laughed.

"So that's a no?"

"That it is."

The club breathed again. Somebody clapped. The DJ played "You Got It Bad" like it was a soundtrack. Big J smiled like he wasn't even mad — just disappointed like a dad at a Little League game.

Before he left, he handed me the chain.

"Still want you to have it."

I took it and tucked it in my boot. And as he walked out, I could hear the DJ talking over the music,

"He gon' cry in the car."

Present Day....

He wasn't just some therapy client with weird kinks — he was that dude. Big J. I was now sitting in a visitor chair next to him waiting for him to wake up. Big J turned over in bed to face me. Initially he looked sheepish, eventually alert.

"You've been playing me," I said, arms crossed. "You knew who I was this whole time."

Jaime leaned back like he was the king of petty.

"And you didn't. Until now."

I stared at him, half mortified, half impressed by the long game he had just pulled.

Three weeks of nonsense. Three weeks of him making me do "therapy exercises" with him like dipping his toes in pop rocks and sucking the powder off. Three weeks of him pretending our sessions were healing his insecurities about his afflictions when the whole time it was really just payback for that night under the neon lights.

"You thought you were slick," Jaime said. "Guess you don't remember how you clowned me, huh? Got the whole club looking at me crazy. You on stage taking bows while I'm walking out taking Ls."

I gave a dry laugh.

"First of all, sir, it wasn't a bow. It was a curtsy. If you're gonna be petty, get the details right."

Jaime's smug grin cracked, just a little.

"And second," I continued, standing up and grabbing my oversized purse, "if you think you won something, remember this — you still paid me for every single minute you wasted."

I snapped my fingers twice for emphasis — snip snip — like cutting a ribbon.

"Congratulation.,"

I walked toward the door, tossing those words over my shoulder like confetti.

"You just pulled off the longest, saddest lap dance in history. You need therapy for real now. Not the kind I give."

Jaime sat there, expressionless, as my heels tapped the sweet rhythm of karma down the hall.

Outside, I pulled out my phone and started a voice memo for my vlog. In the middle of speaking, I noticed a toll-free number coming through. I recognized it as the same number that usually calls when I have done a bit too much spending. That's when my bank calls to ensure there's no fraud. I answer timidly.

"Hello?"

A polite, clipped voice came through the line. Corporate. The kind that always sounded like they were sitting in their office with an ergonomic chair, light roast coffee, and no snacks.

"Good morning. May I speak with Martina Black, please?"

"This is she."

"Ms. Black, this is Cynthia from First Union Bank. I'm calling regarding your account ending in 9311."

"What about it?"

"There appears to be a discrepancy with a recent cash deposit. Nothing serious, but it's something we'll need you to come in and help us clarify in person."

"A discrepancy how? You mean the amount?"

"No, no — the total's fine. It's just a minor flag in the system from our back-office team. Routine, but we're required to verify some things in person when cash is involved."

"Y'all can't talk to me over the phone now about it?"

"Unfortunately, with this type of transaction, it has to be handled face-to-face. Just swing by our Seven

Mile branch — we'll have someone waiting to assist you."

I paused.

"Am I in trouble or something?"

Cynthia gave a soft, rehearsed chuckle.

"Oh, no! This is very routine. We just want to make sure everything lines up before our end-of-week processing."

I let out a small breath of relief.

"Okay... well, I can come down in about an hour."

"Perfect. Just come to the teller window and ask for me. We'll get you in and out."

We hung up.

Something about it felt... off. Had me staring at my phone after we disconnected. Something wasn't right.

I made my way home, changed and got dressed anyway — slick ponytail, black joggers with the gold zippers, fresh hoodie, light beat on the face. Professional enough to say, "I'm grown," casual enough to say, "but I fight if I need to."

When I walked into the bank, Cynthia met me at the window with a tight smile and a clipboard.

"Martina Smith?" she asked, like they hadn't just talked.

"Yup."

"Right this way. We've got a small conference room we're using today."

My eyebrow raised.

"I can't just handle it at the window?"

Cynthia's smile didn't move.

"Oh no. It'll just take a second."

As I followed her past the customer line and into the frosted-glass room, I still had no idea. No clue.

Not until the door clicked shut behind me.

And two plain clothes officers stood up from the table.

One pulled out a badge. The other had a folder.

"Martina Smith?"

"Yeah…" I said, eyes narrowing. "Who the hell are y'all?"

"We're with the financial crimes unit. We have some questions about the cash you deposited earlier this week."

I blinked.

"Excuse me? Y'all brought me in here like I had an overdraft fee — not a damn investigation."

The first cop opened the folder and pulled out a counterfeit bill in a clear sleeve.

"Can you explain where you got this?"

My heart dropped — not in fear, but in fury.

Because this wasn't just some bank issue.

This was a set-up.

This was Jaime.

Fuck.

Tam Telling Tales is a passionate advocate for literacy and the creative force behind the YouTube channel Tam Telling Tales, where she interviews authors, actors, and filmmakers to uncover the stories behind the art. A proud member of the EyeCU Reading & Social Network, Tam has a deep love for historical fiction and meaningful dialogue. While Karma marks her first time as a published author, her true passion lies in sharing stories, amplifying voices, and inspiring others through the power of books, film, and conversation.

Call Me Karma

By

Samaracheré

I was about 10 years old when it happened. My cousin Darious shot my aunt in the face with a 12-gauge shotgun. The memory is as fresh as the day it happened. I remember it all. From Auntie V. calling my mom to tell her what happened. To Mom and I jumping in the whip to get to Aunt V. To Aunt V. sitting on the porch smoking a cigarette with smoke coming out the hole in her face while she waited for the EMS.

I couldn't help but think, that was some G shit fosho. It almost seemed like it was taboo to talk about. I didn't understand why at the time. But what I did understand was, it's always supposed to be family over everything. That nigga failed to live by the code.

One thing was for sure; Auntie was tiny but had the heart of a lion. She took that hit like a G. If nothing else, God was by her side. Many don't survive a hit like that. He tried to take her out, but he helped her become stronger and more ruthless than ever. I vowed by any means necessary, I was going get back at cuz for what he did to Auntie.

I was told I had to help her clean the wound and change the bandages. Being a child, I had no choice. Doing that for months only made my hatred for Darious grow deeper. I watched her as she recovered. Physically, it was not an easy task. Her mouth was wired shut with a brace to keep the jaw aligned. We had to mash meat with a fork to stuff between the wires just so she could eat. That was one sight that would always be ingrained in my head. But to top it off, he wasn't held accountable. There was no jail time, my auntie couldn't even get victim's benefits because of his bullshit. It was a struggle. Soon as I got old enough to make shit pop off I was popping it

They called me lil G. The G stood for Geraldine but, that just wasn't fitting for the streets. So, I shortened it a bit. I was hanging with the swipers, killers and dope dealers and learning the street game from the realest. They only reinforced what I had been bred from. It was what I knew. Momma had me working before she got locked up. The way I cooked up the dope and cut that smack, you would think I was a chef.

One day this fiend came to the spot. I recognized that nigga immediately. It was Darious. My hatred for him was so deep, I felt myself beginning to hyperventilate. I rushed to the back of the spot. My mans and them were looking at me trying to figure out what was going on. But I couldn't focus enough to calm down or let them know what was up.

Darious didn't even recognize me. I looked a lot different than I did at the age of ten. Which ultimately worked in my favor. Seeing him had my blood boiling so bad my whole body was shaking. My man's served him while I was in the back trying to get my shit together.

"Man come on look out fo' yo' mans."

I heard him say. And that's when the plan formulated in my head.

"You good?" Big E asked.

"I'm straight."

He gave me a side eye like he wasn't sure, but I just went about business as usual. Didn't none of them need to know what was up. Another thing I learned from my momma, don't nobody need to know your moves. If they don't know they can't snitch.

A week went by before I saw Darious again. I take that back. I had seen him, he didn't see me. I watched that nigga's moves for a week. I knew where he laid his dirty ass head, what corner he begged on and what little crackhead bitch he called himself married to. But it had been a week since I was in the house when he came to get served. I was standing on the porch when he staggered his stankin' ass up the walkway.

"Damn. Who is you? You a pretty thang."

"Don't worry about who I am. What you want?"

"What can I get for this?"

He pulled out a crumpled up, dingy ass ten-dollar bill.

"Nigga, you think I'm dumb or something. You know what that funky ass bill gets you."

He snickered waving his hands, rocking side to side like crackheads do. All I had was a mean mug for his ass. I wanted to spit in his fucking face.

"You know how it go. I had to try." He laughed again.

"Either get this rock or get the fuck out my face."

"You ain't gotta be mean. Here."

He handed me the bill and I slid him his little baggie.

"Come on you can look out for your mans," he said.

It was like clockwork.

"First of all, you ain't my mans. But I got some new shit I wanna test out."

I pulled out another baggie. It had a blue crystal that almost looked like an uncut diamond. My momma mighta been a hustler and she mighta taught me the game but she was also smart. And one thing she told me was I wasn't gone be a dummy either.

She made sure I didn't fuck around when it came to school. My GPA never dropped lower than 3.5. And my best subject, Chemistry. All the cooking and cutting was part of my chemistry lessons.

"What's this?" he asked.

"Do you really care? It's some shit that's gone get you high."

"I don't do no meth."

This nigga had the nerve to act like a crackhead with standards. But he shot his own momma in the fucking face.

"It ain't meth. But if you don't want it, that's cool. I'll give the shit to somebody else."

"Nah, nah, now. I'll take it."

"You ain't even gotta smoke that. Just let it melt on your tongue. But don't do that shit 'til you get where you going. That shit right there gone have you unable to walk."

"Yeah, alright."

"I'm telling you. It's gone have you too fucked up to walk. Wait 'til you get stationary."

He staggered back down the walkway. I watched 'til he got to the corner. While I stood on the porch leaning against the pillar, I saw his crack wife coming from across the street. She must've been meeting up with him so they could get high together. Before she could get to him, his hand went to his mouth. I couldn't do nothing but smile. Just like a fiend, he couldn't resist. Even better, he wasn't gonna share.

That nigga started dancing. Then he started shaking real hard. I could see his whole body moving from where I stood on the porch. That crack wife of his started screaming. I could see what was happening, it sure did bring a smile to my face. That bitch was just standing there screaming her crackhead ass head off. The next thing you know his fucking head exploded.

"Damn. I didn't expect that to happen."

Samaracheré never considered herself a reader but being persuaded by her best friend to join the EyeCU Reading & Social Network changed everything. Now an avid book lover who devours multiple titles a month, she also serves as the club's dedicated secretary. *Karma* marks her debut as a writer—proof that sometimes the most unexpected chapters turn into the best stories.

Anything For Love

By

T. Denise

Listening to the Waiting to Exhale soundtrack has my emotions all over the place. This is one of the best soundtracks ever.

"I was your lover and your "SECATARY…""

I turned the radio up louder, trying to block out the screams coming from the trunk.

"You messed with the wrong BITCH!!!"

She couldn't hear me, but it made me feel better. Why won't this bitch shut the fuck up? I was also trying to drown out the words that were on replay in my head.

"Niecy, I am so sorry, I never meant to hurt you. I love you like a sister. I was trying to help you. It was your fucking idea!"

Once someone gets caught, they become apologetic and remorseful. She knows that I am not the one to play with. I went to Detroit Central High. If you know, you know. We met in ninth grade and have been inseparable ever since. I considered her my second sister. Whenever you saw me, you saw her. She was "my person" and this shit hurts. We were there for each other's dating drama, miscarriages, and abortions.

In my twenties, I was a little loose. I couldn't take birth control pills and hated the way condoms felt. Having unprotected sex led to several abortions and a miscarriage. As a result, I was told that I was unable to have children, which initially upset me; however, I eventually came to terms with the diagnosis. The doctor said it was due to scar tissue from one of the abortions. I had to look on the bright side to keep from being depressed. I have always wanted to have children, but I guess that was my punishment. I was young and reckless and not ready to be a mother. If only I could turn back the hands of time.

Most of my friends had children so they were envious of me. The absence of children allowed me the freedom to travel without a care in the world. If I wanted to go to Chicago for the weekend, I did. If I wanted to take a spur of the moment trip to Vegas I did. I didn't have to worry about finding a babysitter and shit like that. I also didn't have to ask a significant other if I could go.

Some of the trips were with the girls and some were with men in my stable. I dated a lot of men, but I wasn't looking for anything serious. I just wanted to have fun. Filling my nights with sex, drinking and drugs helped to dull the pain and emptiness I felt inside. There were times when I thought that I wanted a relationship with one of my *friends*. I gave a few of them a try but none panned out to be anything serious.

My girl Bayyinah saw that I was spiraling so to get me back on track she proposed a challenge, or you could say a dare. I have never been one to punk out on a dare and I am always up for a challenge. She dared me to write a book, so that's exactly what I did. I loved to read, and I was very good with words. I wasn't famous but I had a lot of readers. I sold my book online and out of my trunk and at pop up shops. I went to the post office a few times a week to ship orders. I would always see this cute guy buying money orders. I always wondered why people didn't have a checking account. One day I heard, "Excuse me, are you an author?"

"Yes, why?"

"Hi, I'm Curtis, I see you here mailing books all the time. I was just curious. Can I buy a copy? My mom is a member of EyeCU Reading & Social Network. She is always looking to support local authors."

"Wow, I sent them an email and asked if they would consider selecting my book as a book club selection."

"I might have a little pull. I'll buy a copy for her and a copy for myself."

He was licking his lips, so I just smiled and nodded. I'm sure I missed some of the conversation. I was flattered by his interest in me. Standing at 5'2" and weighing two hundred pounds, I was self-conscious about my weight. I considered myself subtly attractive. My big breasts usually grabbed the attention of men.

Curtis told me he owns a trucking company and a few other businesses. The next time we saw each other at the post office he asked me to go to dinner. Despite perceiving him as being out of my league, I quickly said yes. I was hesitant because most men with a lil money are dogs. After dinner we went to Hazel's Place for drinks and dancing. He said it was a hole in the wall. I just laughed and started singing one of my favorite songs, "Let's go baby to the hole in the wall. I've had my best time y'all yes, I did at the hole in the wall." We danced and talked for hours. He told me that he enjoyed my book. I said we could have book club when on our second date when we were sober.

After that first official date we spent most of our free time together. One day he asked me to spend the weekend with him and after that he didn't want me to go back to my place. Three months in he asked me to sublet my townhouse and move in with him. He said it didn't make sense for me to be paying high ass rent at the townhouse and I was never there. He had a point and after approximately six months of living together Curtis proposed to me.

He expressed a keen desire to marry and start a family very soon which presented a big ass challenge. While I was elated by his proposal my inability to have children was a major barrier and I didn't know what the fuck I was going to do.

I was happy, but not happy, happy, happy. I had to give this man a baby by any means necessary. He was an only child and for him this would have been a deal breaker. I had to figure out a way to make his dreams come true. I needed some ideas. I started searching for a Lifetime movie I'd seen where the woman pretended to be pregnant and befriended another pregnant woman in birthing class. She killed the lady and stole the baby. That was some unthinkably crazy shit. I could never do that to someone.

My girl Charlene told me to just tell Curtis the truth. I tried on so many occasions. When I brought up how much I enjoyed the freedom of not being tied down with a child, Curtis' demeanor changed.

"Are you saying that you don't want to have my babies?"

"Of course, not. We should just wait until we're married and just enjoy each other before we start a family."

"I'm down with waiting a year."

I smiled and was relieved that I had bought myself a little time. I laughed inwardly because he was already trying to get me pregnant. I made him wear condoms at first when the relationship was new. I used the excuse that I didn't want him to get me pregnant. After the proposal he said he shouldn't have to wear rubbers anymore. He said he would pull out. Who the fuck did this nigga think he was playing with? Did he think that I was a naive teenager who doesn't know that precum can get you pregnant and that pull-out shit is a set up?

Knowing that I was in a bind and desperate Charlene offered to help. She agreed to be my surrogate. I ordered a turkey baster from Amazon to put our plan in motion. Prime is the shit!

While Curtis was on his business trip we talked every day. I teased him with phone sex. I knew he would be horny as fuck and would want some of this good good as soon as he got home. In preparation, I cooked a great meal. Pork Chops, macaroni and cheese, cabbage, and cornbread. To be perfectly honest, I didn't cook it. My friend Samara cooked it. When Curtis got home he ate and took a shower.

I poured him a glass of White Hennessy with a little something extra. He was so out of it that he didn't even bitch when I made him wear a condom. I sucked him to get him ready. Those drugs had his dick hard as a rock. I must say that I was impressed myself. I rode the hell out of the dick.

He came so hard, I swear he filled the condom. I removed the condom and collected my sample. I was very optimistic. I heard that Golddiggers used this method to trap wealthy athletes. When he left for work I grabbed the condom from the freezer, the turkey baster and headed to Charlene's for the next phase of the plan. Our first try did not work. Maybe it was our method.

I was determined; I came up with another idea. When I told my girl about my new plan, it was easy to get her on board. I was shocked that she didn't protest. Thinking back, she was actually a little too eager.

On this night, I told my man that I wanted to get freaky and of course, he was down. I poured the White Hennessy concoction, rolled a blunt and it was on and poppin'.

I got the blindfold and handcuffs out of my naughty drawer. I sucked his dick something wicked. That was when Charlene came from the closet and switched with me. We had the same build and weighed about the same. She seemed a little hesitant at first but once she saw that pretty dick her mouth watered, and I could see the glint in her eyes. I swear that bitch smirked at me. It felt funny watching my friend have sex with my fiancé. Normally, I would fuck a hoe up for fucking my man. I had to keep telling myself that this was for the greater good. This was to ensure that we had the life and family we wanted. He is well endowed, and every time she went down on his dick she moaned in ecstasy. I prayed that this method worked because I could not do this again.

We waited a week and then we went to the hospital. My friend Monique is a nurse, and she was able to do an early pregnancy detection test for us. The second method worked like a charm. Next, I took her positive pregnancy test home to my fiancé, and he was so excited. He said he wanted to get married right away so his child would not be a bastard. A month later we became husband and wife. Because of our schedules I was able to hide my fake pregnancy easily at first. As the months went by faking this pregnancy was becoming increasingly difficult.

I could tell that my so-called friend was becoming attached to my baby. She was smiling and rubbing her stomach constantly. I reminded her that she was giving the baby to us, and in return I would pay off the mortgage on her condo. She was having second thoughts. She started saying how this was so wrong, and Curtis deserved better. She threatened to tell Curtis the whole story. I couldn't let that happen. We had come too far to turn back. My baby shower was a week away. I convinced her to wait until after the shower before she blew up my fucking life.

She told me the whole plan about how she would show up to the shower in a form-fitting dress to show off her very pregnant stomach. Up until then, she was wearing baggy clothes to hide the fact that she was pregnant. She was already a big girl; there wasn't much hiding she had to do. As for me, I was a big girl too, but

I had to get even bigger to fake the pregnancy. I also was wearing fake pregnant bellies and mastered a pregnancy waddle.

All I'm saying is, I had done too much and come too far for it all to crash down at my baby shower. She ended up not coming to the baby shower. Not to spare my feelings, though. She didn't feel well. It may have had something to do with the laxative I put in her iced tea. Only God knows.

Calm down. The laxative I chose was safe for pregnancy. My baby was unharmed; she was sick as hell and couldn't come to the baby shower. Win-win.

The truth is Charlene changed her mind about going through with our plan because she started having feelings for Curtis. Before she got pregnant with my husband's child, she was always around us, and I was always telling her wonderful things about him. She knew he was one of a kind. I don't know whether it was pregnancy hormones, or she had been having feelings for Curtis all along, but what I did know was that I was willing to kill and or die behind mine. Charlene was playing with the wrong one.

The next day, I went to go check on Charlene. Laxatives taken in excess can be brutal. But she was feeling fine. A little too damn fine. I had a key to her house, and I walked right on through the back way. Charlene was in her living room telling Curtis everything. And I mean everything. Curtis never said anything. He just nodded and "wow"ed over and over. For the first time ever, I couldn't read him. I didn't know if he believed her or not.

"We can be a family, Curtis. This is our baby. We are a family anyway. Might as well make it official. You don't want to be with no lying, conniving, deceitful bitch like Niecy. Look at how I came clean. It's because I can't sleep at night knowing that we lied to you. But Niecy has no remorse about deceiving you."

That was it! That winch had gone too far! I made my presence known and did the only thing there was left to do: cry.

In true Curtis fashion, he ran to console me. After I calmed down, he asked, "Is it true?"

I couldn't lie anymore. This was my chance to come clean.

"Yes."

"So that's why we have to have sex in the dark. You don't want me to see your stomach."

I allowed my silence to be my answer.

"I—I—I just don't know, Niecy. This is a lot for one day."

"I wanted to give you everything like you've given me everything. I stayed up at night for months sick at the fact that I couldn't make you a dad. I had to do something. I love you so much and just want to give you the world. My love for you made me so desperate I was willing to try anything."

"I am hurt, Niecy. You violated me, lied to me, risked my life. Did you even make sure she was clean before I had raw sex with her?"

Again, I let silence be my answer.

"I'm clean! You ain't gotta worry about that!" Charlene interjected.

"Okay."

Curtis redirected his attention back to me.

"I love you. And only love can make you do something this stupid and off the wall. I'm flattered, I guess."

"No! She's a liar, deceiver, and a crafty bitch. You cannot trust her! Choose me before she lies to you about anything else. Before she sets you up again," Charlene pleaded.

Before I could say anything, Curtis looked at me.

"Let's kill her and take the baby. She's far enough along. The baby will be alright."

"Let's do it," I answered without a second thought.

Charlene took off running as fast as she could, but it wasn't fast enough. Curtis was an athlete, and Charlene ran like she was nine months pregnant... because she was. Curtis easily overpowered Charlene. We hogtied her, stuffed kitchen towels in her mouth, and threw her into the trunk.

"Follow me in your car," I told Curtis.

I drove to our cabin in Holland, Michigan. Thought it was best to let her go into labor naturally, then kill her. But Curtis wanted her gone as soon as possible. The way he saw it, the longer she was alive, the greater the chance Charlene had of getting away. She would snitch. We couldn't have that. She was a loose end, and he hated loose ends.

As we were deciding what to do, Charlene went into labor. The stress of what was going on probably helped that happen. After she gave birth to our beautiful baby girl she was no longer needed. Curtis gutted her like a fish and I helped him throw her body in the lake behind the cabin. We would forever be bonded by this secret. Our love had been tested, and we passed with flying colors. Now, the three of us could live happily ever after.

T. Denise is an original member, former Vice President of EyeCU Reading and the founder of Precise Editing Services, where she helps authors refine their work with care and precision. A first-time author and lifelong avid reader, Tina brings a deep love for storytelling and a sharp editorial eye to every project. Her passion for literature and dedication to uplifting fellow creatives make her a valued force in the literary community.

Karma Ain't Kind

By

Kaylynn Hunt

2020…...

"Are you ok?" Sharon questioned.

Veronica was doubled over in pain, her knees buckled and she nearly dropped to them.

"I…don't…. know," she dragged out between ragged breaths.

"Come have a seat."

Sharon tried to help her to one of the armchairs that sat in the front section of the company restroom. Just as they reached the chair, Veronica attempted to grab the arm of it. At the blink of an eye, Veronica toppled over.

"HELP!" Sharon called out kneeling next to Veronica.

Helen, another of their co-workers, pushed the door open then asked, "What's going on?"

"Call 9-1-1." Sharon immediately stated.

Helen ran back out of the bathroom. Sharon assumed to retrieve her phone or get security. By the time the ambulance arrived, Veronica had begun to come to.

"What happened?" Veronica questioned, her voice raspy and faint.

"You passed out, honey. Don't try to get up, an ambulance just arrived."

Veronica tried to sit up anyway, her head was spinning and pounding. She rested back on the floor placing her head on the folded-up blazer Sharon had positioned for her.

The EMTs came in, did their assessments, asked questions all the while getting her on the gurney. They were about to roll her down the hall.

"Here, I grabbed your phone and purse," Helen said as she sat the things next to her.

"Thank you."

As soon as she got the phone in her hand, she pulled it out to dial Terrence. She listened as the phone rang and rang and rang until she heard the voicemail greeting. She hung it up thinking he'd call her right back.

By the time they arrived at the hospital, Terrence still hadn't returned her call. She called again to no avail. She then shot him a text letting him know that she'd passed out at work and had been transported to the hospital. Now, here she was admitted, and he still hadn't responded. She didn't know whether to be pissed off or worried.

Terrence

"Go ahead and answer that bitch's call," Niecy stated, full of attitude.

"Why the fuck are you worried about my phone? You need to be worried about putting this dick in your mouth."

Terrence finished his statement as he grabbed Niecy by the back of her head, pressing it to his crotch. Just as the tip of his shaft hit the back of her throat, his phone began going off again. This time he didn't even bother to look at it. He shut it off. Nothing was going to ruin this good nut he was about to let go down Niecy's throat.

Niecy did just as she was told, she always did. Terrence was a fun toy for her. She didn't care that he had a girl. She was always calling, and he always ignored her. The attitude Niecy appeared to have was as fake as Terrence's relationship. But if Terrence could play a game, so could she. When they first met, she thought he was charming but the more she got to know him, the more she realized who he really was. Yeah, he gave her the spiel about having a girl but not being happy. When she inquired as to why, he would give some vague or trivial reason.

Six months ago, she bought his bullshit. But the more bullshit he spun, the more familiar it became. Same bullshit she'd been through before. That's why her faith in relationships had long gone out the window. Now, she was just like poppa, a rolling stone. When she finished with Terrence she had a date with Jacob. Marvin was lined up for the next day and the list went on. So, no she really didn't care about Terrence's ringing phone. But he should've.

Veronica sat in the hospital bed in tears. Terrence had yet to call her back, nor answer a text. The more she thought about it, the more pissed off she became. There she was sitting in a hospital bed reevaluating her entire life. Too embarrassed to call anyone else, she sat alone in her thoughts. How could she face anyone telling them Terrence was nowhere to be found. She was done giving him the benefit of the doubt. This wasn't his first time being M.I.A.

All the things that they'd fought about, replayed in her head. All the times he'd said he cherished her, went out the window. Because as she lay there watching the I.V. drip, waiting for answers, she thought about how in the times when she needed Terrence, he wasn't there. But this time was pivotal; she could be dying. Hell, she could be in surgery right now and he wouldn't know it. The scales in this relationship were far from balanced.

"Ms. Walker." The doctor entered the room, interrupting her thoughts.

"Yes."

She wiped the tears from her face giving him her full attention.

"I do have some answers for you."

"What did you find?"

"Well, you have what is known as PID, pelvic inflammatory disease. It can be treated. Given the severity of this, we'll begin antibiotics intravenously. We'll have to monitor you for a few days to ensure surgery isn't necessary."

"What is the cause of it?"

"PID is caused by a number of factors but one of the most common— untreated STDs in your case, gonorrhea." Veronica took in a sharp breath at the realization of what he said. "The antibiotics will take care of that as well. You will need to contact any sexual partners you have had."

"There's only one," she stated through gritted teeth. "I want to be tested for everything."

"We did that." Veronica's response was just a nod. "The good news is, this can be treated, and this isn't something that will stick with you for life."

Veronica's blood was boiling with so much anger, her tears had evaporated.

The vibration of her cell phone interrupted the churning of thoughts in her head. When she looked at the name that flashed on the screen, she felt relieved.

"Hello," she answered with a bit of venom and sadness.

"Bitch, what the fuck is wrong with you?"

Tamara, her best friend, was probably the only person in the world she would confide in.

"I'm in the hospital."

"What? Why the fuck didn't you call me? Where? For what?"

Veronica closed her eyes as she began recounting her day to Tam. Having to say out loud what she'd been told, caused the tears to fall once more.

"I'm on my way," was all Tee said before hanging up.

One Week later……

"You don't have to do this," Veronica said.

"Yes, I do."

"I can stay at my own house."

Veronica sat in the passenger's seat of Tamara's SUV amused at her friend's antics. It was at her insistence that Veronica come stay at her house for a few days. Though Terrence didn't know she had been in the hospital, he'd tried calling. His call didn't come until the day after she was admitted, it went unanswered. As badly as Veronica wanted to cuss him out from that day to two Sundays to come, she knew it would be in vain. Her point was proven when the health department had contacted him to tell him to get treated.

Terrence left her a voicemail calling her every name but her given one. His reason was that she was the cheater; she'd infected him. They both knew that wasn't true. When Veronica didn't respond to him with the energy he'd expected, he turned to apologizing and pleading.

"Nah, when I went by your house to check on things, there were roses at your doorstep."

"His begging won't work this time."

"I'm here to make sure that shit sticks. I've heard that before. I don't know if that niggas dick is made of gold or not, but I know it's dirty. And he ain't playing on your emotions on my watch."

"Tam, my number is changed, locks changed. I'm good."

"Your address didn't. That's why you're coming with me. That nigga knows he better not come to my doorstep."

"I want to lay in my own bed."

"Ok, then I'll come stay with you."

"I don't need a bodyguard."

"Refer back to my previous statement."

"Tee, I know it's hard to believe. But even if giving me something wasn't a non-negotiable trying to turn the shit around on me sure the fuck was."

"I mean I still got my brother on ready. We can have the nigga's ass beat."

"He's not worth the jail time."

"If you say so."

"My lease is up in a couple months. What are you going to do? Live with me until then?"

"If I fucking have to."

"Bitch! I'd be ready to kill you."

"I'm just saying."

"Trust me when I tell you, I'm done with him. Help me look for places to move. Two months and I'm out. No more Terrence with the golden dirty dick."

Presently…...

Terrence woke up and couldn't move. He was still a little groggy from the night before. He smiled to himself when he thought of what transpired. His whole body ached. Terrence was still in disbelief at the turn his night had taken. Until last night, he hadn't seen Roni in five years. When he saw her everything in him tingled. At that moment he wished he hadn't played games with her. Veronica looked beautiful, just as she always had. But her body seemed to have improved. Not that there was anything wrong with her body before, but she'd gained some pounds in all the right places. At first, he wasn't going to speak. He wasn't sure what kind of response he'd get, after all things didn't end very well with them. He watched for a while from across the bar and admired the features of all the women who accompanied Veronica.

No matter how much he tried to ignore the group his eyes drifted back over in their direction. If he could just catch Roni's eye he would be able to gauge whether or not he had a shot at a conversation. He wanted to tell her all the things that he was sorry for and actually mean it this time. Terrence decided his best bet was to turn on the charm that won her over the first time around. So, he called over the bartender and directed him to buy all the girls a round on him. Once the drinks were placed in front of them, they were pointed in Terrence's direction.

Roni looked up to see, who she still thought was the sexiest man alive, staring back at her. She blushed. He still had the power to pierce her soul. She raised her glass, nodded then turned back to her friends. They all turned to look at him then seemed to have a hushed conversation that involved him.

"What's so funny ladies?" Terrence asked as he walked up behind Veronica.

"We were just discussing how sexy you are," Roni said as she turned to look at him.

"You think that?"

"Always have."

"Who are your friends?"

Veronica introduced him to everyone then ordered more drinks. They all had light conversations. Terrence couldn't help but stare at Roni when she smiled. He always loved her smile. The more they drank the more they flirted. It got later in the day, drinks flowed, conversations on keeping the party going got started. Somehow, everyone ended up at Terrence's home, having their own party. As much as Terrence liked to boast about changing, he was reveling in the fact that he had five bad bitches in his house. His mind wouldn't stop moving trying to figure out how he could conquer all of them. They were all beautiful and stacked. If he hadn't spoken to all of them at length, he would've sworn they all danced at the same club.

One thing led to another, then all his dreams come true. It started out slowly. Two of them, SanTasha and Lucinda, began kissing each other. Terrence walked up behind Laura as she swayed her hips. They were all dancing together when clothes began to come off. Veronica sat back watching everything go down. She imagined this was the type of thing he was doing behind her back when they were together. Some anger began to creep up her spine. There was a little sadness mixed into that, he was never the man she thought he was. She quickly shook off the feeling. It was time to enjoy what was going down.

The activities escalated as the clothes came off. Terrence wasn't sure who to focus on or what parts needed more of his attention. By the time he'd passed out he'd sampled all the goods. Now, he stood in the bathroom mirror smiling at himself. The room kept spinning so he decided to stagger back to bed for a little while. He'd obviously drank a little more than he should have. But he wouldn't take it back. He'd had the time of his life.

Once seated at the edge of the bed, he noticed the note sitting on his nightstand. Terrence chuckled thinking how Roni hadn't changed. She used to always leave him sweet notes and gifts before she left. He smiled, picking up the note. As he read, his smile began to fade.

Terrence,

      Thanks for last night. It gave me closure. I was so angry at you before. You had me thinking I wasn't good enough for you. I know the problem was you. I can't fix you. Just so you know the girls had a great time with you. I told them that dick was everything. I bet you didn't even notice that I didn't have sex with you last night. While I did enjoy watching you perform. I gathered much greater pleasure knowing SanTasha has hepatitis B, Lucinda is HIV positive, and I hope Laura wasn't having an outbreak last night.

Enjoy your life (or lack thereof)

Roni

Kaylynn Hunt is a founding member of the EyeCU Reading & Social Network, where her love of storytelling and community first took root. As an author, she proudly shares that EyeCU's members were her very first ARC readers—an experience that helped shape her path as a writer. With a passion for narratives that explore justice and consequence, Kaylynn's contribution to *Karma* embodies the chilling thrill of karmic retribution.

Thank You for Reading *Karma*

We hope these stories leave their marks on your heart.

Your time, your imagination, and your emotional investment mean everything. If you enjoyed this journey, we'd love to hear from you! Reviews help authors grow and help readers like you discover their next favorite read.

Leave a Review

Please leave a short review on Amazon, Goodreads, or wherever you purchased the book. Just a few words make a huge difference.

Join the EyeCU Reading & Chatting **group on Facebook**

Stay engaged and connected with all things books. We'd love to have you become a member of our online book club.

From our hearts to yours—thank you.
See you in the next story.

With love,
EyeCU Reading

Discussion Questions

1. Which story was your favorite? Why?
2. Which was your least favorite? Why?
3. Of all the stories, who was your favorite character? Least favorite?
4. Do you believe in Karma?
5. Have you experienced Karma? Bad or Good?
6. Which story delivered the best Karma?
7. Which story shocked you the most?
8. Would you read more from these authors?